THE DEVEREAUX LEGACY

CAROLYN HART

THE DEVEREAUX LEGACY

CAROLYN HART CLASSICS

With a New Introduction by the Author

59 John Glenn Drive
Amherst, New York 14228-2119

Published 2013 by Seventh Street Books™, an imprint of Prometheus Books

Cover image © Ocean Photography/Veer
Cover design by Jacqueline Nasso Cooke

Inquiries should be addressed to
Seventh Street Books
59 John Glenn Drive
Amherst, New York 14228–2119
VOICE: 716–691–0133 • FAX: 716–691–0137
WWW.PROMETHEUSBOOKS.COM

17 16 15 14 13 • 5 4 3 2 1

Library of Congress Cataloging-in-Publication Data

Hart, Carolyn G.
The Devereaux legacy / by Carolyn Hart.
p. cm.
ISBN 978-1-61614-704-4 (paperback)
ISBN 978-1-61614-705-1 (ebook)
1. Haunted plantations—South Carolina—Fiction. 2. Cousins—South Carolina—Fiction. 3. Family secrets—South Carolina—Fiction. I. Title.

PS3558.A676D48 2013
813'.54—dc23

2012040720

Printed in the United States of America

INTRODUCTION

Looking back to previous books is an odd experience for an author. I remember reading about a panel that clever British author Joyce Porter once described. When panelists were asked whether they ever reread a book once it was in print, Joyce Porter and all the panelists but one responded absolutely not.

The exception was a male author who described picking up earlier books and whiling away hours in delight. Joyce Porter commented that once you've written the first of however many drafts, rewritten to an editor's suggestions, copyread the MS, and proofed it, the idea of rereading the book at a later date for pleasure was unthinkable. Or, as I would put it a trifle more tartly, you would have to be out of your ever loving mind!

However, I will confess to a bit of fun in looking at some books that are now going to reappear almost three decades after they were initially written.

The Devereaux Legacy is one of these books. It reflects a day before cell phones and constant linkage to the world. It was, in fact, much easier for an author to thrust a heroine into danger. Now, when the heroine is cornered by the villain, she whips out her cell and dials nine-one-one.

The Devereaux Legacy also reflects a bit of my past as a writer. In the late seventies, there was very little interest in books by American women mystery authors. New York believed in two kinds of mysteries, the hard-boiled private eye books written by American men and traditional mysteries written by dead English ladies.

I was a writer living in Oklahoma (as I still do) and I had no contact with New York. I attended writer conferences in hopes of gaining some understanding of why the kind of books that I had been writing and selling were no longer finding a publisher. During this period, I wrote seven books in seven years and during that time sold none of them.

Finally, the path seemed clear. Romance novels were Queen. You couldn't sell a mystery. You had to write romance.

I took an idea for a mystery, added what I hopped would be an appealing romance, a ghost who may presage evil, and a beautiful old South Carolina plantation. The result was *The Devereaux Legacy*, which sold to Harlequin as a gothic romance.

I hope today's readers will enjoy returning to that slower-paced world and I am grateful to Seventh Street Books for making this adventure possible.

Carolyn Hart

CHAPTER ONE

Leah looked up at the cross-topped steeple, then pushed through the iron gate in the old brick wall east of the church. The brick walkway, smoothed from years of use, led to a side door. She was nearing her goal after a long journey, both in space and in time. Her hand tightened on the Dhurrie purse her grandmother had given her for Christmas. It contained the fragment of the last letter her grandmother had ever written and the much-read magazine article that had brought Leah to this small town in South Carolina.

She climbed three shallow steps and opened the side door. A golden pool of light spilled out from an open doorway midway down the hall. A typewriter clicked rapidly.

Leah hesitated for just an instant. She was so near now. Soon, she would know the truth. The article must have been wrong. It must have been. Still, it took every ounce of will to go forward, to walk into the office.

A plump middle-aged woman with tortoise-shell glasses and a generous smile looked up and paused in her typing. "Hello. May I help you?"

"Yes, please. Can you tell me where the Devereaux graves are in the churchyard?"

"Of course." The woman turned and picked up a large stiff-backed book from the shelf behind her. She thumbed through the pages, then stopped. "The Devereaux family graves are in the oldest part of the cemetery. Here, let me show you on the map—"

Leah watched as the plump finger pointed out the path that would lead her to the graves.

"Thanks. Thanks very much."

"If you have any trouble, you can ask one of the gardeners."

Leah found the graves eventually. It was dim and still in the old part of the cemetery. Spanish moss hung in thick gray swaths from the live oak trees, creating a shadowy enclave of moss and lichens among the age-worn stones that carried the name of Devereaux. But it was not these stones she sought. They didn't constrict the breath in her throat and make her heart thud erratically. The stone she sought was a thin sheet of shiny granite carved in the shape of a sailing sloop. It glimmered in the dim light that filtered through the glossy-leaved live oaks, looking like a ghost ship sailing toward a murky horizon.

Leah stared at the names incised upon it:

Mary Ellen Devereaux Shaw, Age 24, Lost at Sea

Thomas Marquis Shaw, Age 28, Lost at Sea

Leah Devereaux Shaw, Age 2, Lost at Sea

Louisa Abbott Shaw, Age 59, Lost at Sea

She reached out a hand to touch the shiny granite, so warm from the August heat. But that warmth couldn't touch the iciness in her mind. Not many people ever stood and touched a gravestone that bore their name—for she was Leah Devereaux Shaw.

Why was her name there? What did it mean? Who had ordered this memorial in the belief that she had died at sea?

Died at sea? Part of it was true, or so she had always thought. Her mother and father had been lost at sea. That was what Grandmother had told her. Grandmother Shaw. Louisa Abbott Shaw. And why was her name listed there, too? She certainly hadn't perished at sea. She'd died one month before, in Rockport, Texas, and been laid to rest in the graveyard of St. Luke's Episcopal Church. This graveyard was in Mefford, South Carolina.

Although cicadas whirred in the heavy August heat, Leah still felt cold. She would have bet her life on Louisa Shaw's honesty and integrity, but this stone memorial proved that Louisa had lied to her. Not once, but over and over again.

Leah had grown up believing that her parents had been lost in a hurricane in the Gulf of Mexico, off the Texas coast. She'd never heard a word about South Carolina.

Not one word.

She stared at those names cut into the granite and felt incredulous—and betrayed. Why had Louisa lied? Or was this stone a lie? Why had Louisa never told her of Mefford?

Leah opened her purse and took out Louisa's last effort to communicate. It still hurt her to look at the letter, because the words were so frightening, so unlike Louisa, and because that sudden sharp splotch of ink signaled the end of a vital and loving life. Louisa had suffered a massive heart attack as she'd written the letter, and Leah had found it when clearing out the house several days after the funeral.

> Dear Carrie,
>
> You will believe this is a voice from the grave. I can't expect you ever to forgive me, but I feel that I must write. By chance—or perhaps Providence—I came across the article about The Whispering Lady. Oh, dear God, Carrie, if the ghost walks again, it means I was deceived that night. It means that evil . . .

And that was all. That, and the article that had been roughly torn from a magazine, an act so foreign to the meticulous and orderly woman.

Leah had read and reread those few sentences, then the page torn from the magazine. It described the reappearance of The Whispering Lady, one of the South's most famous ghosts, seen again after an absence of many years at Devereaux House in Mefford, South Carolina.

Even now, standing in the dim and isolated part of the cemetery, Leah remembered the shock she'd had on seeing her family name in print. Worse was to come because the story emphasized that The Whispering Lady returned only when a Devereaux was fated to die. The article recounted her appearances over the years, including the time just before the daughter of the house, Mary Ellen Devereaux Shaw, and her husband, Thomas, had been lost at sea.

But it wasn't tales of ghosts that had brought Leah to Mefford. It was the totally unexpected link to South Carolina.

Suddenly, a lizard skittered over Leah's sandal. She gave a little cry and jumped back. The lizard, surely as frightened as she, sped away, diving into a tangle of creepers and weeds. A little haze of dust and a deep smell of rot shimmered in the hot air. The lizard had disturbed an old gravesite that had lain hidden beneath subtropical growth for many years.

She didn't take it as an omen. She didn't believe in omens. Or in ghosts. Yet she felt that Louisa's heart attack had been triggered by the magazine article.

No, she didn't believe in ghosts, but she'd traveled a long distance to lay some ghosts to rest herself. How had her parents died? And why was her name on that granite memorial?

Leah shivered again, though the air was thick and heavy, hot as spongy asphalt.

Abruptly, she swung around and hurried back to the brick path that led out of the cemetery. At that moment, she wanted to leave it all behind. Deep inside, she was afraid. If Louisa had lied to her, lived a lie, there must have been a compelling reason. She'd been a good, kind person who'd always done her best for Leah. Leah knew that her grandmother had loved her; she had no doubts about that at all. So, if Louisa had lied . . .

From beneath the dappled shade of the live oak trees, Leah came out into the side street. The heat pressed against her, and she felt enervated. Perhaps she'd drive directly back to the airport at Savannah and fly home to Texas. Leave the past alone.

Her hand was on the door of the green Vega she'd rented, when she looked across the street and saw a white frame building. It was the Mefford Historical Society. Leah hesitated. Maybe she should try to find out something more about the Devereaux. The magazine article had said that the Devereaux family—her family—had been part of Mefford for many years.

It was pleasantly cool inside the building. A woman sat behind a counter to the left of the door, absorbed in a book, her vividly red hair falling softly about her face. Leah turned to the left, drawn by the pamphlets stacked on a table. As she glanced at the piles of pink, yellow, green and white brochures, she had an inkling of the importance of the past to this little town. Some of the titles that caught her eye were Battle Sites, The Thompson House, A Guide to Historic Beaufort and Sheldon Church Ruins.

She picked up a small white booklet, Historic Mefford Homes, and found the listing for Devereaux Plantation. The picture of the house showed it glowing creamy white in the late-afternoon sunshine. It had a high, stuccoed foundation, and two sets of steps mounted to the first-floor veranda. Wrought-iron railings framed the steps in graceful arabesque curves. Leaded windows sparkled in the fanlights. Sleek Doric columns supported the second-story veranda. The house was a magnificent symbol of an era long past, yet fascinating in the reality it reflected of another age. Leah could imagine a carriage turning up the oyster-shell driveway, carrying an elaborately gowned woman and her escort. She could almost see their faces. . . .

Absorbed in the photograph, she began to read the history of Devereaux Plantation, skimming over facts and years. Claude Devereaux had brought his sixteen-year-old bride to Mefford in 1711, the year the settlement had begun. The house they'd lived in was one of the oldest low-country mansions and was still inhabited by the Devereaux family.

Leah had come to South Carolina to find out the truth about her parents. She'd discovered their names and her own inscribed upon a gravestone. Somehow, it had never occurred to her that she might have living relatives. She was so much an orphan, so accustomed to thinking that the only family she had in the world was Louisa, that she had never expected to find any living kin.

She looked down at the booklet and turned to the back of it to study the map. There was no Devereaux house on it, but a footnote offered the information that the house was four miles outside town, on the Mefford River.

Dazed, Leah took the booklet and another brochure containing a history of Mefford and went over to the counter. The redhead still sat there, immersed in her book. She wore a lovely lilac dress that emphasized her fair skin.

"I'd like to buy these pamphlets," Leah said and opened her purse to get some money.

The woman reached out for the booklets, revealing a heavy gold bracelet on one wrist and fingernails that were painted a dark red. "That will be seven dollars and fifty cents. Would you like . . ." As she looked up, she drew her breath in sharply and stared at Leah with widened eyes. Shock flattened her face, making her seem suddenly old. Still staring, she repeated, "That will be seven dollars and fifty cents."

Slowly, Leah found the money, then asked breathlessly, "Who are you?"

Almost fearfully, the redhead replied, "I'm Cissy Winfrey." When it became apparent that her name meant nothing to Leah, she glanced away and picked up the book she'd been reading.

Leah hesitated, but the woman ignored her. Yet she knew she hadn't imagined what she'd just seen. Her face had shocked Cissy Winfrey. Should she challenge her and demand an explanation of her odd behavior? The woman would probably shake her head and look puzzled, and Leah would be turned away. Reluctant to appear a fool, she headed for the door and opened it. On her way out, she glanced back and saw the redhead reach for the telephone.

Outside, the heat struck her with a physical force. She felt heavy and languid, as though she moved in a dream. She walked slowly back to the car and rolled the windows down farther, waiting a few moments before climbing in. She knew why she was taking so long, drawing out the time. She wanted to go to Devereaux Plantation, but she was afraid. She didn't belong there, no matter what her name was. She was an intruder, back from the grave, like a lost spirit seeking its earthly home.

Irritably, she started the Vega and lurched out into the street. At the stop sign, she looked again at the lovely old church, then glanced at the street sign. Beaufort Drive. The tour of historic houses began here. She opened her guidebook, read for a moment, then turned right, knowing she was delaying the time when she must decide whether or not to go to Devereaux Plantation.

But the drive had a thoroughly unexpected effect on Leah. She hadn't planned on falling in love with Mefford. That wasn't part of her carefully reasoned plan. Yet the homes she passed struck her with delight. They weren't mansions, at least not to the eyes of a Texan, but were sturdy clapboard and brick buildings, surrounded by moss-hung live oaks, magnolias and weeping willows. Leah was charmed by their stately porticoes, their elegant wrought-iron fences and gates, their lush, fragrant gardens.

She drove up one street and down another, picturing other days and other lives. On Cornwall Street, she admired a small but perfectly proportioned two-story house with upper and lower verandas. A glance in the guidebook told her that this was one of the oldest houses in Mefford and belonged to the Winfrey family.

Winfrey. That was the name of the red-haired woman at the historical society. Leah's feeling of uneasiness returned.

The tour ended at the LeClerc house, which had a garden open to tourists. Leah pulled up to the curb, hesitated, then got out of the car. She was still delaying making a decision about going to Devereaux Plantation.

She pushed through a creaking gate and walked down a brick path. Crape myrtle masked an old wall. Honeysuckle spread along an iron fence. Banks of azaleas followed the contours of the gently sloping ground. The whole effect was of a natural woodland, an enchanted semitropical glade, heavy with fragrance, dim and shaded in the quiet of a summer afternoon. A wasp hovered near the honeysuckle. Leah slapped at a mosquito on her bare arm.

It was so dim in the shade of the live oak in the center of the garden that she didn't see the elderly lady coming, her soft-soled slippers slapping noiselessly against the path.

"No trespassers here," a reedy, high voice warned. "I have my pistol, and I'll shoot it."

Leah looked up, startled. "I'm sorry," she said quickly. "I thought the guide book said the garden was open to visitors."

The woman wore a faded, shapeless cocoa-colored dress. She leaned on her cane, and her wizened face split in a grin. "Everybody thinks I'm a crazy old lady. But I have a pistol." She thumped her wooden cane for emphasis, then peered nearsightedly through the gloom. "My, you're just a girl, aren't you? Perhaps I'll take you inside and show you my mirror that belonged to Empress Josephine or the inkwell that George Washington gave to my great-great-grandfather." She drew nearer to Leah. "Perhaps I'll even show you—" Her eyes squinted at Leah, and her words broke off sharply. She poked her head forward. "You, girl, come out of that shadow."

Leah hesitated. Mrs. LeClerc swung her stick forward and tapped Leah's arm. Slowly, Leah stepped out into a patch of sunlight, standing close enough to the woman to see the question in her dark brown eyes.

Mrs. LeClerc touched Leah's arm with a claw like hand that had no more warmth or substance than a feather.

"Blood tells," she said huskily. "Bad blood and good blood. There's no getting away from it." Then, almost angrily, she asked, "What are you doing, tramping around my garden, pretending to be a stranger?"

"I am a stranger."

Mrs. LeClerc thumped her cane pettishly. "My husband was cousin to the Devereaux. I've spent a hundred evenings in that drawing room."

Leah shook her head and shrugged her shoulders.

For a moment, the surety in the woman's eyes faded, and she looked puzzled. "You don't know what I'm telling you?"

"No."

"Then I'll say it plain, young lady. Yours is a fated face. There's been love and hate and death, and no one knows what happened, no one. They tell me, too, that The Whispering Lady walks again at Devereaux Plantation. You'd best beware." She took a deep breath and sagged against her cane. "I'm tired now. I'll go in."

Leah watched her until she disappeared inside the house.

A fated face. What could that mean? Leah had no idea, but she realized she couldn't slip into Mefford and not be noticed. Yet she had every right to be there if she wished, no matter how much she might look like these Devereaux whom she didn't know.

Abruptly, she made her decision. She was going to visit Devereaux Plantation.

CHAPTER TWO

Devereaux Plantation.

The words had a ring of magic. Her name. Her people. As the Vega picked up speed, Leah felt a tingle of excitement. Soon she would be meeting kin, bone of her bone, flesh of her flesh.

But why had she spent all those years in Texas believing she was an orphan with no living relative other than Louisa? Why had Louisa hidden her family from her?

She slowed the car, searching for the side road to the house. The apprehension she had felt in the cemetery returned. Perhaps she was foolish to seek out these Devereaux. The elderly Mrs. LeClerc had said, "Yours is a fated face."

Leah glanced up at the rearview mirror and smiled a little at her reflection. She looked the same as usual, her black hair a little unruly with its thickness and curl, her eyes a matching color, her face a bit thinner as a result of her grief over Louisa's death. Normally, a laughing face. But she hadn't laughed much these past few weeks.

Fated. That word carried with it a dark and haunting message.

Just a few yards ahead, Leah saw the turnoff. She hesitated, then, almost angrily, wrenched the steering wheel, and the little car plunged onto the narrow, rutted track.

Every shade of green gleamed in the dusky tunnel formed by the overlapping branches and the vines that swirled up tree trunks. Delicate ferns, spiky stalked plants and tuberous runners carpeted the spaces between the trees and edged sinuously out onto the dirt road. Leah drove slowly, feeling as if she were trying to swim underwater in a silt-heavy lagoon. The underbrush and vines shimmered and waved like seaweed, creating a murky, ominous atmosphere.

The road twisted again, and gates loomed ahead. Leah stopped the car and got out to open them. They were warm to the touch and moved grudgingly. She drove the Vega through, then got out again to shut the gates. In the overpowering heat, that small exertion tired her. Her blue cotton dress clung to her, and she paused to rest for a moment.

The road curved sharply to the right, running along the river. Through scattered pines she could see a double row of live oaks and knew they formed the avenue that led from the river up to the house. At the end of that road, atop a long rise, she glimpsed patches of slender white columns and two huge brick chimneys. Brightness flashed against her eyes. She looked a little to her left and saw, separate from the house, a brick tower with windows at its top.

A yellow Porsche bucked to a stop only a few yards from her Vega, angling across the narrow road and blocking the way to the house. The driver's door swung open, and a stocky blond man climbed out. The emphatic click that filled the air as he shut the car door was a crisp reminder that his car blocked her way.

Leah glanced over her shoulder. She was hemmed in by the closed gates behind her and the car in front of her. No breeze moved in the pines; no sound emerged but the man's quiet footsteps.

Was it the heavy silence of the alien countryside that imbued him with menace? Or was it just Leah's sensation of being trapped? She stood frozen with fear beside the Vega.

He halted a few feet away and stared at her. His face was a curious mixture of expressions—shock and dismay and something else she couldn't quite identify. Then he shook his head. "I can't believe it!"

Leah knew that once again her face had revealed her. She lifted her chin and said determinedly, "I'm Leah Shaw. And I've come to see Devereaux Plantation."

He waited a long moment before saying, "Leah Shaw's dead."

Her birth certificate was in her purse. She fished it out and handed it to the man.

He studied it, his face furrowed in concentration. He was fortyish and handsome in a heavy-featured way. When he handed back the certificate and looked at her, his expression was frankly hostile. "Where did you come from?"

What business was it of his? "Who are you?" she returned sharply.

His light blue eyes flickered. "You don't know?"

"How should I?"

He shrugged. "You've come here."

"I saw a magazine article. My name was in it—and my parents'. It said they sailed from Devereaux Plantation the night they were lost."

"Is that all you know?"

Leah nodded. "Who are you?" she repeated.

"I'm your cousin, John Edward Devereaux."

"Really and truly my cousin?" she asked wonderingly.

"If you are Leah Devereaux Shaw."

"I am."

He frowned. "But where have you come from? Where have you been all these years?"

"I grew up in Texas, in a little town on the Gulf. I lived with my grandmother."

His head snapped up. "Your grandmother? That's impossible!"

"My grandmother, Louisa Shaw."

"My God." He shook his head like a boxer stunned by a hard blow. "This is incredible. We thought she was dead, too." He leaned forward, his eyes cold and intent. "What did Louisa tell you?"

He called her Louisa. That meant he knew her. Leah felt as if she were walking in the dark and missing a step. Louisa had known she had this cousin—and others?—but had never told her. Why?

"Louisa didn't tell me much," Leah said carefully. "She said my parents drowned when I was a baby—that they'd been on a sailing holiday in the Gulf and were lost in a hurricane."

"In the Gulf?" He looked puzzled. "There was a hurricane, but it was in the Atlantic. Their yacht, The New Star, sailed from here." He paused, then added quietly, "It was exactly nineteen years ago today."

"I didn't know that."

"But if Louisa never told you about Devereaux Plantation, then how did you find your way here?"

Leah told him calmly enough, but her voice reflected her pain. "Grandmother had a heart attack in her study. Later . . . I was straightening up her desk, and I found a magazine article and a letter she'd begun."

"A letter? A letter to whom?" He waited tensely for her answer.

"She was writing to someone named Carrie."

The man drew his breath in sharply, and Leah knew he recognized the name.

"Who is Carrie?" she demanded.

He stared at her for a long moment, his eyes as unreadable as shiny glass. Then, reluctantly, he said, "Carrie is Mary Ellen's mother."

Mary Ellen's mother. Shock constricted Leah's chest. Mary Ellen was her mother, so Carrie had to be her grandmother. Leah turned and stared up the hill at the elegant old home. Nothing had prepared her for this. John Edward continued to talk, yet the sound of his voice seemed to come from far away. Her grandmother . . . A quick thought darted through her mind, that her grandmother was dead. But Carrie would be her other grandmother, the grandmother she'd never known. The wonder of it caught at her heart.

"But you do understand, don't you?"

Leah looked at him blankly. What was he saying?

"It would be too much of a shock for you to burst in on her—"

"Hey, John Edward!" The shout carried clearly in the hot, still air.

A man walked confidently down the road. Tall and slim, he carried himself with grace and self-assurance. In the rich flood of afternoon sunlight, his hair gleamed like polished copper above an aquiline nose and a generous mouth. He moved toward them commandingly, but as he came closer, he stopped in his tracks.

Once again, Leah knew it was her face that held him captive.

A fated face. Whatever the old woman had meant, Leah knew now that her face indeed meant something to those who lived at Devereaux Plantation.

But what?

Then the man moved forward and stared boldly down at her. She backed away a pace from the intensity of his scrutiny.

"She says she's Leah Devereaux Shaw." John Edward's voice came from behind her.

"I am Leah Devereaux Shaw."

The newcomer still stared at her, his dark blue eyes electric with energy. Then he shook his head, like a man who couldn't believe what he saw. "In the dining room there's a portrait of Mary Ellen." His voice was deep and musical. "Now I see that portrait before me. The same eyes, dark as the sky at midnight. The same hair, glossy as ebony. But Mary Ellen's been dead for nineteen years. Where have you come from?"

Leah wished suddenly that she and this man could have met another way, that they could have come together without the tendrils of a hidden past entangling them, because she had a sense of estrangement from him even though they had yet to meet formally. She knew that this mattered to her and would matter in ways she couldn't even understand.

She tried to ignore the past, just for the moment. "Who are you?" she asked.

"I'm Merrick Devereaux."

She shouldn't have been surprised. She should have expected it, but still she felt a deep, almost aching wrench of disappointment. Merrick Devereaux. He must be her cousin. Leah did not want him to be a cousin.

"Merrick Devereaux . . . my cousin?"

"Yes, I'm your cousin."

"If she really is Leah," John Edward put in.

Leah still held her birth certificate in her hand. Without a word, she offered it to Merrick. Her hand touched his. It was such a small contact, so meaningless in daily life, but this time it was special. Was he as aware of her as she was of him?

Before he bent to look at the certificate, his glance once again touched her face. For an instant she thought she saw a flash of excitement, but it was almost immediately obscured by puzzlement and worry.

Why was she causing so much distress? These cousins seemed not only astounded by her appearance but also disturbed.

Merrick's gaze moved from the paper to her face. The shock in his eyes was still there. He handed back the birth certificate. "I don't understand. All these years we believed that you died on The New Star with your parents and Louisa."

Again she told her story, sparse as it was, adding that her grandmother had a little antique shop in Rockport.

"Louisa alive." Merrick's blue eyes darkened. "It's unbelievable. Incredible! Why didn't she get in touch with us? How could you and she have survived the hurricane, and Mary Ellen and Tom have been lost?"

Leah had no answers, only questions. She reached out and touched his arm. "John Edward said my other grandmother, my mother's mother—"

"Carrie," Merrick said.

"Is she alive?"

"Oh, yes." His face was unreadable now.

Leah looked up toward the plantation house. Her Grandmother Devereaux was there. She took one step, then another.

A hand reached out and gripped her elbow. "You can't go up there." John Edward's heavy face loomed over her, furrowed with disapproval.

She pulled away from him. These men, her cousins, stood between her and Devereaux Plantation. Why were they so determined to keep her from reaching the grandmother she'd never realized she had?

"You can't keep me from her. I'm going to—"

John Edward again moved between Leah and the house. "Do you want to kill her? She has a bad heart, you little fool. You can't burst in on her and—"

"It's too late." Merrick's voice was even, uninflected.

"Too late?" Leah's voice rose in distress.

Merrick swung toward her, but his hand was warm and gentle against her arm. "No, no, I'm sorry. I didn't mean anything had happened to Carrie. I meant that she knows you're here. Mrs. LeClerc called and told her that she found you walking in her garden."

Mrs. LeClerc. The little old lady in the cocoa-colored wrapper, who'd said Leah had a fated face.

Merrick looked at John Edward, and when he spoke again his voice was expressionless. "Aunt Carrie's been standing on the front steps ever since with her opera galsses. She saw Leah's car turn in and sent me down to fetch her."

CHAPTER THREE

Devereaux Plantation gleamed a delicate creamy white in the soft light of the late-afternoon sun. The house was much larger than Leah had imagined from its picture in the guidebook, the double set of verandas broader, the Doric pillars heavier. Even so, it was subordinate to the old woman who stood at the top of the steps, a tiny figure in a gray silk dress. Her thin white hair was pulled back into a bun; her frail hands were clamped to a silver-headed cane. The woman's expression was stern as she watched Leah climb the steps. But in her huge dark eyes were mirrored the hope and the anguish in her heart.

"Leah."

The voice so faint she scarcely heard it.

"Leah, oh, Leah." Carrie Devereaux's mouth quivered, and tears slipped down her crumpled cheeks. She raised her arms to clasp Leah to her. Leah smelled the clear, sweet fragrance of violets and felt the wraithlike touch of her grandmother's arms. She held the tiny figure close, her eyes brimming with tears.

The old lady reached up and touched her face. "Oh, dear God, you are the image of Mary Ellen." She smoothed back Leah's dark hair and traced the shape of her face. "After all these years of sorrow, I can't believe you're here." Abruptly, anger flashed in those dark eyes so like Leah's. "Who has kept you from me? Why have I never known you?"

She turned on Merrick and John Edward.

"What kind of conspiracy has done this to me?"

Alarm flashed in John Edward's eyes. He looked at Merrick.

But Merrick moved confidently forward, reached out and touched her arm. "Now, Aunt Carrie, you know we had nothing to do with it.

We don't understand it, either, but apparently Louisa took Leah away."

"Louisa." The old lady's hand tightened on the silver-headed cane. "Tom took Mary Ellen away, and Louisa took Leah." Her face was terrible in its anger. She jerked back toward Leah. "You must tell me. I must know."

Leah stepped back a pace. She understood that the woman's anger sprang from a terrible grief, yet she couldn't permit anyone to be ugly about Louisa.

"I don't know what happened. I don't know why Louisa took me away, but she loved me. I do know that. I'll always know that."

"Loved you. And she must have hated me."

"No, oh, no. Louisa never hated anyone. And she was writing to you when she died."

"To me?" Carrie Devereaux stared piercingly at her, then addressed Merrick and John Edward. "Go now. Leave us. I must talk to Leah alone."

She took Leah inside, down the large central hallway and into the cool dimness of the library, thumping her cane on the polished wood floors as she went. After seating herself in a wing chair near the fireplace, she motioned Leah to sit opposite her.

They stared at each other across a gulf of time and pain.

"Well?" Carrie Devereaux said finally.

Leah told her everything she knew. When she'd finished, there was another long silence.

Carrie Devereaux leaned forward. "The letter Louisa wrote—do you have it?"

Leah took the letter out of her purse and handed it to her grandmother. While she read it, Leah looked around the room. Red cedar bookshelves lined two of the walls from floor to ceiling. A Sheraton table held a brass clock. Hepplewhite chairs sat against one wall. Satinweave upholstery in a robin's-egg blue covered a claw-footed sofa. A hand-tufted rug lay in the center of the room.

The old lady finished the letter and placed it on the low tea table in front of her. "All these years I thought that you and Louisa and Tom and Mary Ellen were lost on The New Star. All these years." She stared at Leah, her dark eyes huge and bewildered. "What happened to them? Tell me that!"

Impulsively, Leah reached across the tea table and took her hands. "I'm so sorry. I wish I knew. And I don't understand, either, because Grandmother—" she meant Louisa, and Carrie Devereaux knew it œ"—was always so kind and so good. I don't know how she could have kept us apart. I just can't imagine what happened."

Carrie Devereaux said emptily, "If only I'd been here."

Leah frowned. "You weren't here?"

The old lady shook her head. "Pride can carry you through mighty bad times, Leah. The Devereaux have always had that kind of pride and the fine courage that goes with it. But sometimes pride grows ugly and puffs you up and turns your head the wrong way, and misery will follow you." Her huge dark eyes fastened on Leah. "Misery's been following me for a good long while now." She squeezed Leah's hands, then clutched the head of her cane. "I haven't seen your mother since before you were born, and I'd never seen you. Louisa knew that. She must have thought I wouldn't want you after whatever happened here that night."

Leah drew back a little. "If you hadn't seen my mother in so long, then why were we here?"

"Because Mary Ellen loved her old fool of a mother." Carrie sighed. "Mary Ellen was such a happy person, never sullen or quarrelsome. But she had a very strong will." The old lady smiled a little grimly. "I daresay she came by it honestly enough. And she loved your father very much. She had written twice, asking to come. Finally, I wrote back and said she could visit—alone. She never answered that letter. You were only a baby then."

"Why didn't you like my father?" Leah heard the stiffness in her voice.

Carrie lifted her head and looked away, as if looking back through the years. "Tom Shaw was a fine young man, from all reports. Oh, it all goes back to pride, that terrible pride of the Devereaux. Both mine and Mary Ellen's." A faint spot of color touched her cheeks. "Yet I always wanted the best for her." She looked beseechingly at Leah. "That was what I wanted. And she defied me." Her voice rose. "You see, I had chosen the man I wanted her to marry. It was all arranged. The wedding was scheduled for the following September."

"What happened?"

"She was on her way to college on the train, and she met Tom Shaw, who was going back for his second year in law school. She wrote me about him, how odd it was that they should meet on the train. His family had moved to Atlanta after the war, but she knew the name of course, because of our Marthe." Carrie looked at her granddaughter quizzically. "Have you read about Marthe?"

Leah nodded. Marthe's story had been the heart of the magazine article she'd found in Louisa's desk with the half-finished letter. Marthe Devereaux had fallen in love with Timothy Shaw in the summer of 1860, but West Pointer Timothy Shaw didn't come home to South Carolina until late the following year, as a member of the invading Union forces. Then one spring night Timothy came by moonlight to Devereaux Plantation. The next morning his body and Marthe's were found in the old tower, both dead by gunshot. No one ever knew what happened, but ever since, The Whispering Lady had been glimpsed in the Devereaux gardens when death was near. The ghost was seen when Albert Devereaux and his family went down on the Titanic and when The New Star sailed away.

"Just a story, of course," Carrie continued. "But Mary Ellen thought it was such a coincidence that she and Tom should meet and like each other so much, right from the start."

She was quiet for a long moment; then, in a weary voice, she told the rest of it. For the first time, Leah had a picture of what kind of person her mother had been. She'd been beautiful and happy, but determined. Then, shockingly, the day had come when her smiles hadn't prevailed. Caught between the need to please her mother and her love for Tom Shaw, she had twisted and turned, not quite able at first to rebel openly, writing to Tom, the wedding date drawing nearer and nearer.

She had run away a week before the wedding.

"I never saw her again," Carrie Devereaux said.

Mary Ellen had tried twice that summer after her runaway marriage to Tom to see her mother. Each time she'd been turned away at the door. For many years now, Carrie had endured the hell she had fashioned.

Dismayed and puzzled, Leah asked, "Why did they come on The New Star when they knew they weren't welcome?"

"Old Jason was our butler then. He helped me raise those children." She paused, and her eyes saw scenes from long ago. "Oh, what happy times they had, the four of them! You see, my husband's brother, Andrew, and his wife were killed in a car wreck when John Edward, Cissy and Merrick were small, so they came to live with us. Mary Ellen grew up with her cousins, and Jason treated them like his own, but in his heart he was always a little partial to Mary Ellen. He deferred to her, told me she was the smartest and the toughest. So when he was worried, I supposed it was natural for him to write to her rather than turn to the others. He wrote and told her she had to come, that The Whispering Lady'd been seen—and that I was in danger."

"The Whispering Lady," Leah repeated.

Carrie Devereaux's mouth thinned. "All nonsense, of course. A story fit for guidebooks and newspapers. Nothing to it at all. But Jason worried Mary Ellen."

Leah frowned. "Why should he think you were in danger?"

The old lady thumped her cane on the polished floor. "Anyone can have accidents."

"You had accidents that summer?"

"The brakes in the car," Carrie said vaguely. "And I took a tumble down the main stairway." Her mouth twisted. "But death didn't come for me. Not for me."

Jason hadn't told Carrie what he'd done until the afternoon The New Star was expected.

Angry, she'd packed a suitcase and left. When The New Star sailed up Mefford River to Devereaux Plantation, she'd been on the road to Charleston for two hours.

"I always thought," she said, each word came slowly, painfully, "that if I had stayed, if I had been here and welcomed them, The New Star would not have sailed on and been caught in the hurricane." She picked up Louisa Shaw's letter with a hand that trembled. "But you and Louisa survived the hurricane. What happened to my daughter and Tom? For God's sake, Leah, what happened?"

Leah stared into her grandmother's eyes and saw fear and the beginnings of horror. She could only shake her head helplessly. Louisa had known what had taken place that stormy night, but now she, too, was dead.

For the first time since she'd come to South Carolina, Leah wondered if she'd been unwise to make the trip. She had destroyed old certainties and substituted an agonizing puzzle in their place.

"And here Louisa says that she was deceived that night—that if a ghost walks again, there is evil. Then the letter breaks off. Leah, whatever can she have meant?"

Evil . . . growing, spreading, enveloping them all.

Leah looked at Carrie, so old and frail, so tiny in the huge chair, and suddenly she was glad she'd come. "Grandmother," she said quietly, "tell me more about The Whispering Lady."

Impatience flickered in Carrie's black eyes. "It's nonsense. I don't believe in ghosts."

"Neither did Louisa," Leah replied. "But when she read that The Whispering Lady had been seen again, she was afraid it meant danger for someone."

Carrie shook her head. "No, it's just a sad story from long ago." She pointed to a portrait above the mantel. "That's your great-great-grandfather, Julian Devereaux."

It wasn't a fine portrait. Leah could sense the artist's rush; the strokes were hurried, the colors uncertain, but the overall effect was of a greater pathos in the young face beneath the plumed officer's hat and in the narrow shoulders in Confederate gray. She was beginning to recognize the features of her kin: huge dark eyes, high-bridged nose, narrow chin.

"Julian was next in age to Marthe. They were both very much

under the thumb of their oldest brother, Randolph. Everyone said later that she must have done it because of Randolph. He was so very bitter about any Southerner who fought for the Union."

"Must have done what?" Leah asked.

Her grandmother looked at her in surprise. "I thought you'd read the magazine article."

"I did."

"Of course, it doesn't come right out and say it."

"Say what?"

"That Marthe shot and killed Timothy Shaw, then put the pistol to her heart and—"

"Oh, no!" Leah cried. She hadn't read the story that way. She had imagined a slender young girl, walking in the garden, dreaming and hoping and grieving, but she hadn't imagined a twisted loyalty that put political allegiance ahead of love.

"Not a happy story," her grandmother said soberly. "It isn't surprising that no one ever speaks of it. But when things aren't mentioned, there are always whispers, and they breed imaginings. So when the moonlight touches a tree trunk or marsh gas flickers, someone sees Marthe. I'm sure that's how the rumors began that the garden was haunted. In Mefford, they said that generation of Devereaux was doomed. Marthe was a suicide by her own hand. Randolph was killed a few months later when his horse threw him. Even Julian didn't survive the war for very long. He was weak and ill when he came home. His wife, Edith, tried hard to save him, but he died the next summer just before their son, James, was born." The old lady looked up at the portrait. "As he was dying, he kept saying that it wasn't right that Marthe was buried in unhallowed ground by the tower, and he begged Edith to see that her grave was moved to the family plot."

"Was she reburied? Put next to Julian?"

Carrie shook her head. "No. Her grave's just to the side of the tower. Maybe the rector refused. Or maybe there was simply a lack of money."

She smiled at Leah's look of surprise. "There wasn't any money.

Everything was ruined and gone, the land parceled out to freed slaves, the ships seized by the Yankee blockade. Nothing was left but the house, and it had gone to ruin. The windows were broken, the books in the library had been stolen, and most of the rooms were closed off because there was no one to clean them. A little vegetable garden remained. Somehow Edith managed to feed James and pay the taxes. But she lived long enough to see Devereaux Plantation restored. James left South Carolina as a young man to prospect for silver in Colorado. He didn't find any silver, but he did find a wife, Abigail Morris, whose father owned a good deal of the Western American Railroad." Carrie Devereaux smiled dryly. "They do say she was a bit long in the tooth, but James was a good husband."

"And the Devereaux prospered?"

"Oh, yes. James bought back all the land that had been lost, but so many of the levees had been destroyed that he switched from rice to short-staple cotton."

"And no one saw Marthe again until—"

"It isn't Marthe," her grandmother retorted sharply. "It's just a story. The tale went around after Albert and his family went down on the Titanic, but that was just silly babbling by an old maid who wanted attention."

"And the summer my mother died?" Leah asked determinedly.

"Marsh gas."

"Tell me, Grandmother."

The appellation came so naturally. Carrie Devereaux felt that, and it pleased her. "Lilac's my maid, a superstitious old fool. Not that she'll admit it. But I see her turn the other way when she comes upon John Edward's black cat."

"What did Lilac see?"

The old lady shrugged. "Who knows? Something white in the garden. Could have been anything—one of the younger maids slipping out to see a boy-friend. But she told me, and when I just laughed, she told Jason."

Three days after Lilac had seen something, the brakes had failed in Carrie's car. A fast driver, she'd topped a hill and was starting down when a wagon pulled onto the road. She braked—and there were no brakes. A rickety truck loaded with farm workers blocked one lane; the cart, the other. At the last instant, she swerved to her right, toward the reed-thick marshy water, swollen at high tide. The car, a huge Chrysler sedan, hung for an instant in space, then plummeted into the channel, throwing Carrie out into the water. A teenager had jumped from the back of the truck and dived into the channel, staying there until he had found her and brought her up.

It had been, Leah realized, very nearly a deadly accident. No wonder Jason had been worried.

"What happened the second time the ghost was seen?" she asked.

A month later, Jason himself had seen something luminous in the depths of the garden and told Carrie. Later that very night, a faint cry had roused her. She'd thrown on her robe and hurried down the hall. The cry came again, and she'd started down the stairs. That was all she remembered. They found her, hours later, unconscious at the foot of the stairs.

"I fell," she insisted. Then she said wryly, "But even if there is a ghost, it isn't coming for me." She looked triumphant. "The ghost's been seen twice this summer—and not a single thing has happened to me."

"Is this summer the first time the ghost's appeared since The New Star sailed?"

The old lady shrugged. "I think so. But you'll have to ask John Edward or Cissy to be sure. I didn't come back until this spring."

"Come back?"

Carrie Devereaux shook her head. "I keep forgetting you don't know anything about us. Yes, Leah. After all hope was given up for The New Star, I left Devereaux Plantation and went to Nice. I lived there until this spring."

"You just came home this spring?"

Carrie nodded.

"Why?"

Her grandmother's black eyes looked at Leah steadily. "I'm a very old woman. I want to die where I belong." She smiled, a mirthless, twisted smile. "Perhaps there is a Whispering Lady who appears when death is near. Perhaps . . ."

"No, Grandmother. Stop that. I haven't found you to lose you."

But Leah wondered. Not about ghosts, but about an evil that could spread and engulf and destroy.

CHAPTER FOUR

"Henry, show Miss Leah to Miss Mary Ellen's room." The old lady looked up at her with such love and happiness that Leah impulsively bent down and kissed a wrinkled cheek.

"Grandmother, I'm so happy we've found each other. I don't know why we had to be apart all these years, but we will make up for lost time. We will."

As she followed the butler from the library, Leah glanced up and down the central hallway, but it lay empty, the late-afternoon sun shining on the heart-of-pine floor. She fought away a sharp sweep of disappointment, then wondered at herself. Why was she looking for Merrick? Her cousin Merrick. He hadn't been overjoyed at her coming. Why now, as she walked through this strange house and up the central stairway, should her every thought be attuned to him and what he thought of her?

He was her cousin, after all, so of course she didn't really care. There was no reason to. But where was he?

In her room—her mother's room—she stood for a long moment after the door had closed behind Henry. It was a spacious, airy corner room with windows on two sides and a screened door that opened onto the veranda. The pale gray wallpaper held a muted rose pattern. Fresh-cut roses filled a cut-glass vase on the mantel over the fireplace. But the marble-top table by the canopied bed and the marble-top dresser lay bare. Had cosmetics and powder and lipsticks been scattered across them when her mother had lived here? Leah reached out and touched a solid cherry wood bedpost. She had no real sense of Mary Ellen, of her life or her death.

Leah shivered. Would she ever feel at home in this house?

To drive away the dark thoughts that hung over her like the miasma above a swamp, she unpacked, then sat down at the upright desk in the corner and wrote down the bewildering occurrences of this very special day. When she'd finished, she added these questions: What happened to my mother and father? Why did Louisa lie to me? Did a ghost walk at Devereaux Plantation? Why were John Edward and Merrick upset when they saw me?

Leah put down the pen and walked over to the window. The sun was beginning to set, and the Mefford River lay below, a shining stream of silver.

Merrick Devereaux.

Why did her heart have this sudden, different feeling when she thought of him? He was, after all, just a man. No, he wasn't just a man, an inner voice said quickly. He was different from any man she'd ever known—and she wanted desperately to know him better. When would she see him again?

As the red glow from the setting sun crimsoned the windowpanes, she began to dress for dinner. She would never have admitted to anyone that she chose her dress very carefully, a shantung silk of blue shot through with a dark green thread. She hesitated for a moment before the dressing-table mirror, then fastened a choker of pearls around her neck. Her mother's pearls, Louisa had said when giving them to her on her sixteenth birthday.

Leah brushed her hair until it glistened like polished ebony. Carefully, she applied a faint pink blush to her cheeks and a touch of coral to her lips. Then, unsmilingly, she studied her reflection: a rather thin face with high cheekbones and dark, dark eyes; a slender white throat. Would Merrick notice her tonight? Would he be there?

Henry knocked on her door shortly before seven. "Miss, if you will come down to the library now. The family is gathering there."

Slowly, a little reluctantly, she descended the central staircase. The family. That would be her grandmother, of course. And perhaps John Edward and Merrick. Were there others she had yet to meet? How would they greet her?

She felt a moment of panic when she stood in the open doorway to the library. Too many faces turned toward her, but her grandmother, in the wing chair near the fireplace, held up a welcoming hand, and Merrick came over to escort her inside.

"That's a very lovely dress," he said, smiling. "It reminds me of Venice in the moonlight."

"Thank you, Merrick." A surge of happiness moved within her; then she tried to suppress it. He was her cousin. She walked on toward her grandmother.

"Leah, Leah," the old woman said softly. "You know, it was nineteen years ago that Mary Ellen left us. I had been feeling so unhappy, and then you came. Now I am happier than I have been in years." She looked around the room, and her voice carried to every corner. "Leah has been restored to us. We will celebrate tonight."

Leah glanced up and saw everyone still staring at her. With a start, she recognized the red-haired woman who had looked so shocked when Leah had bought the pamphlet at the Mefford Historical Society. The woman's face held no expression now. It was as smooth as a pond on a windless day.

A long silent moment passed after Carrie Devereaux's proclamation. No one in the room, other than Carrie, looked happy or festive. Instead, Leah felt a tension that stretched as tight as a drawn bow. Even Merrick, despite the warmth of his greeting, seemed disturbed.

Maybe she had imagined the faint frown on his face, because he quickly called out, "Come now, Leah, it's time to meet the rest of the clan." He led her across the room to stand in front of the redhaired woman. "This is Cissy."

Cissy was not only the same woman who had been at the historical society but was also John Edward and Merrick's sister.

"Yes, I saw you today." Leah held out her hand.

Slowly, Cissy took her hand and shook it. The heavy gold bracelet on her arm glistened in the soft light from the nearby lamp. Her nails were long and blood-red. Tonight she wore a pale pink silk dress.

"Why did you come to the historical society?" Her voice was pleasant enough, but her eyes watched Leah sharply.

"I'd been to the cemetery, and I hoped to find out more about the Devereaux."

"Do you actually intend to tell us that you had no idea about the family?"

"None."

Cissy made no reply, but she looked skeptical.

Leah flushed and almost challenged her, then realized it would be rude, at the very least. To bridge the stiffness, she asked quickly, "Do you work for the historical society?"

Cissy drew herself up and lifted her chin. Her tone was icy. "I don't work anywhere. I am a volunteer, of course. The members of Mefford's finest families give their time to preserve our heritage and protect it from those who have no knowledge of the past and no appreciation for it."

John Edward tried to put a good face on it. "Cissy's our contribution to historical preservation."

"And, of course, the Winfreys are one of the very oldest families in town," Cissy continued coldly. "You haven't met my husband."

Leah turned toward the slender blond man who stood beside Cissy.

"This is my husband, Hal Winfrey. Hal, this is—Leah."

As she held out her hand, Leah realized how much Cissy hated to accept her, to give her a name and a reality.

"I'm very glad to meet you," she told Hal, whose hand was as limp as cooked cabbage.

He nodded, not so much in an unfriendly way as indifferently.

"It means everything to me to be here," she said. "I thought I had no family in the world now, and to find you, Grandmother, and my cousins—it's wonderful."

"And wonderful for us, too," Carrie said happily. Then, slowly, the joy seeped from her face. "But it does mean that we don't know the truth of what happened when The New Star left here."

Everyone seemed frozen for a moment in the sudden silence that descended. No one moved or spoke, and all eyes were fastened on Carrie Devereaux. The tiny old lady studied first Cissy and Hal, then John Edward, then Merrick.

"All of you were here that night," she said finally.

Leah studied them, too. Cissy was sleekly lovely and expressionless. John Edward seemed more somber than usual. Merrick was sober-faced. Only Hal looked unaffected by Carrie's words—and not terribly interested, either.

But her cousins were interested. And underneath that interest, Leah thought she detected a current of fear.

"Something dreadful must have happened," Carrie said heavily.

John Edward pushed himself up from his chair and crossed the room to stand before her. "We don't know that, Aunt Carrie. This girl's come here with some cock-and-bull story—"

"John Edward," the old lady interrupted sharply, "look at Leah. Just look at her."

He shrugged. "All right. I see the family resemblance. But who knows what the truth is? Maybe the yacht broke apart, and Louisa and Leah were the only survivors. Maybe Louisa lost her memory. Maybe that's why she ran off to Texas. Maybe she just went crazy."

"My grandmother wasn't crazy," Leah said firmly. "Louisa was as sane as anybody I've ever known!"

"Then why don't you know anything?" he demanded. "Why are you a stranger to us?"

"Hush, John Edward. Can't you see the child is trembling?" Carrie took Leah's hand.

Leah held her grandmother's hand tightly, but she continued to stare at John Edward. "I don't know why Louisa never told me, but whatever reason she had, she meant to help me. And in her last letter, the one to Grandmother Devereaux, she said she must have been wrong about what had happened that night."

It was abruptly silent again. This time Leah felt herself shrink inside. Now the silence was dark and inimical and dangerous.

"What d' you know!" Hal exclaimed wonderingly. "This is damned interesting. What did the old girl say in the letter?"

Leah felt a wave of revulsion. Up to this moment, Hal had been so ineffectual, such a handsome nonentity, that she'd ignored him. But now his air of bored indifference was gone. He looked brightly curious, the kind of ghoulish curiosity that passersby exhibit when tragedy strikes.

But she answered him because the others waited, too, waited with a taut intensity to hear what she would say.

"Louisa saw that article on Southern ghosts, the one that described The Whispering Lady. Then she sat down at her desk and started a letter to Grandmother." Leah nodded toward Carrie Devereaux. "She wrote that if the ghost had been seen again, then she was wrong about what had happened that night. It meant there was evil at Devereaux Plantation."

Evil at Devereaux Plantation. The words hung, stark and ugly, in the air.

Cissy leaned forward, one hand gripping the edge of her chair. "Then what?"

"That's all. She must have had her heart attack while she was writing the letter, because the pen scrawled off the page. . . ." Tears burned in Leah's eyes. She could imagine the sudden wrenching pain, the moment of knowledge, then nothingness.

"How dreadful," Cissy said faintly.

John Edward was shaking his head. The skeptical look in his eyes angered Leah, but she kept quiet. It would do no good to quarrel with her newfound cousins. Then she glanced at Merrick. He didn't look hostile or angry or worried. He looked kind.

"So you see," Carrie Devereaux said in a dry, brittle voice, "we must try and discover what really happened that night."

Cissy turned toward her. "But, Aunt Carrie, how can we? That was nineteen years ago."

"I know that," the old lady said stubbornly. "But all of you were here then. I want each one of you to think back, to remember exactly what happened. Tomorrow night after dinner, we will work it out together. Tomorrow night we will remember." She lifted her chin. "But tonight we will celebrate Leah's return."

Carrie led the procession into the dining room, leaning on Merrick's arm. Cissy and Hal came next. Leah noticed the almost imperceptible check on herself that Cissy made as she turned to take the seat at the head of the table. Leah was beginning to sort information out in her mind, picking up one fact here, another there. Cissy and Hal had lived at Devereaux Plantation ever since their marriage, and Cissy had been mistress of the house during her aunt's long sojourn in Nice.

The dining room was of a piece with the rest of the house. A centerpiece of yellow roses adorned the elegant Sheraton table. A matching sideboard was resplendent with shining inlays of satinwood and ash. A chandelier hung from the center of a huge plasterwork medallion set into the high ceiling. Its crystals glistened and swayed in the light breeze coming in from the open windows.

There was no air conditioning at Devereaux Plantation. The house was designed, with its broad main hallway, to catch the prevailing breezes. The huge windows on either side of the dining room fireplace were bare, their velvet drapes taken down for the summer. Above the mantel hung a portrait of Mary Ellen, a young and smiling Mary Ellen with dark brown eyes and black hair blowing in the wind. She wore a white decollete dress and the same pearls that Leah wore this night. What kind of evil had troubled that smiling, carefree face? Leah wondered.

It was an awkward meal, despite the excellent and unobstrusive service and the wonderful shrimp creole with red rice. But they all watched one another without seeming to.

Leah was fascinated by her three cousins, especially by Merrick. She liked the way he tilted his head when he listened, the hearty burst of his laughter, the blunt firmness of his chin and the softness in his dark blue eyes when he looked at her. She thought he was extraordinarily attractive.

He talked to her throughout dinner, and she felt much the same as when she drank champagne—excited, happy and a little bit dizzy.

"Tell us about Texas," he urged.

She laughed. "No one can describe Texas in an evening."

"The wide-open spaces and all that?" John Edward prompted.

Leah didn't like his tone. She looked at him coolly. "I'm a Texan by adoption, I guess. In Texas, it matters more what kind of person you are than who you are." Then she looked uneasily at her grandmother. She didn't want to offend, and she'd realized in only one day in Mefford that here it mattered terribly who you were.

But Carrie Devereaux was smiling.

John Edward and Cissy weren't smiling.

Leah knew they resented her. She wasn't welcome at Devereaux Plantation, despite her grandmother's smile and Merrick's warmth.

However, Cissy did make an effort to be polite toward the end of the meal. "Do you ride, Leah?"

"I haven't for a while."

"We still have several good horses. We'll plan a ride one day soon."

Again, discomfort swept over Leah. Did they all assume she'd come to stay? She hadn't had that in mind at all when she'd left Texas. But what did she have to return to? A house emptied by Louisa's death; a job in a travel agency. Yet what would hold her here? Her newly found grandmother, of course. Somehow she couldn't imagine eating in this magnificent dining room night after night, talking to people she didn't really know, becoming part of a life so different from what she'd known.

But Carrie Devereaux was her grandmother, and Merrick, John Edward and Cissy were her cousins.

She looked at them again—at Cissy with her glorious red hair, at John Edward with his Scandinavian fairness, at Merrick with his deep blue eyes and richly auburn hair. Then, as she had done so often during the meal, she looked up at the portrait of her mother. Studying it, she understood Mrs. LeClerc's shock when she had seen Leah in her garden. The portrait might have been of Leah herself.

Leah wasn't paying any attention to Hal, Cissy's husband, who sat across the table from her. Despite his good looks, Hal seemed to fade quickly from his surroundings. So she was startled when he spoke to her. "It really is amazing."

Leah understood at once what he meant. He had noticed her staring at the portrait. He looked over his shoulder at it and said again, "It really is amazing."

Everyone at the table glanced at the portrait, then at Leah, whose face flushed with embarrassment.

"It's an incredible likeness," Hal prattled on. "Blood lines are like that, you know. Why, I've got a bitch now who's whelped two champions that look just like her. Blood tells."

That was what Mrs. LeClerc had told Leah.

No one said anything. The silence, a tense, brittle silence, unnerved Leah, and she hurried to fill it.

"Thank you," she said quickly. Then she added, "She was so pretty." She flushed a deeper red because she realized that it sounded as if she were complimenting herself. She stumbled on. "But I wasn't thinking about whether I look like her. I was fascinated by the resemblance between this portrait and the one of Julian Devereaux in the library. You can tell we all belong to the same family. Yet it's interesting how the same family can have such decided differences."

They all looked at her blankly.

"I mean, I'm so dark, and my mother was too, and Grandmother. We all have eyes that are almost black. Yet the three of you—" she meant John Edward, Cissy and Merrick "—are so much fairer and have light eyes."

She knew she'd said something terribly wrong. They looked stricken, appalled. The makeup on Cissy's face stood out in purplish splotches. John Edward's mouth was a thin, hard line.

Merrick came to Leah's rescue. "You've mentioned the unmentionable." But he said it gently. "No one ever alludes to the fact that we are Devereaux through adoption, not blood. Andrew Devereaux, the younger brother of your grandfather, married our mother after she'd been widowed. So that's why none of us has the Devereaux coloring."

"Oh, I'm sorry," Leah said quickly. Then she flushed again when she realized how that sounded. "I mean, it doesn't make any difference."

"Of course it doesn't make any difference," Carrie Devereaux said emphatically.

Oh, but it did. It took all of Leah's willpower not to laugh, not to jump up and clap her hands. Merrick was not her cousin. By law, by his place in the family, yes, he was her cousin. But he was not a blood relation. The delight she took in his nearness, the happiness that welled within her when their eyes caught and held—they were right.

The awkward moment that followed was smoothed over when her grandmother began a long description of the fall gala held annually at Devereaux Plantation and how Cissy managed it so well.

Leah listened and nodded and spoke occasionally, but all the while she was thinking. Of course it made a difference—in another way, too. After Mary Ellen's death, her adopted cousins would have become the heirs of Devereaux Plantation. Now that she, Leah, was back from the grave, what would her grandmother do? Surely that question had occurred to them. They couldn't know that she had no designs on their inheritance.

She almost spoke up to say she hadn't come to Devereaux Plantation to make any kind of claim. But even to bring it up would sound forward and grasping. She would have to make it clear to her grandmother in some appropriate way, that under no circumstances would she come between her adopted cousins and what they had been led to believe was rightfully theirs.

Leah was grateful when dinner finally ended and they went into the drawing room for coffee. Despite the grandeur of the moldings and the center medallion, the room was made cheerful by the light and graceful chairs, mostly Chippendale, and by the cream-colored wallpaper with its blue forget-me-not pattern. She found the atmosphere relaxing and welcoming.

When she sat down with her coffee in a corner of the room, next to an eighteenth-century secretary, Merrick joined her.

"Don't be upset," he said with a smile. "It really doesn't matter."

"I didn't mean to say the wrong thing."

"You didn't, Leah, believe me."

She felt a glow of pleasure, different from any she'd ever known. His eyes were deep-set, and she knew she could lose herself in them completely. With an effort, she looked down at her cup and took a sip. Then she asked, "What do you do, Merrick?" and was proud of how casual she sounded.

"I'm a farmer. Mostly, I take care of all of Aunt Carrie's land."

"Do you enjoy it?"

For an instant, his easy smile slipped away, and he looked very serious, almost grim. "It's the only life I've ever wanted." He stared down at her, his brows drawn close together. Then, slowly, his expression smoothed out. "Would you like to see the plantations, Leah?" He asked it almost hesitantly. "I'd like to show you everything—if you'd be interested."

"Of course I'd be interested."

Pleased, he leaned forward. "Do you like it here?" When she didn't answer immediately, he shook his head. "Sorry. That was a dumb question. You've been here less than twenty-four hours, so—"

"I love it," she said firmly. The strength of her answer surprised her.

He looked delighted. "You feel the magic, don't you?"

She nodded. "I think I do, Merrick, I think I do. It's a sense of time, a feeling of peace. I feel . . . I feel at home." She looked around the stately room. "It's so different from anything I've ever known, yet it seems so familiar, so right."

"That's because you do belong here. And now that you've come home, you're going to stay for always."

His gaze held hers, and once again she felt that sweep of emotion. She wondered what it would be like to touch his hair, to hold his face in her hands. The thought both shocked and delighted her. And, her heart sang, Merrick was her cousin by adoption, not by blood at all. That gave her the license to enjoy this new and exciting feeling.

He held out his hand. "Come on, Leah, let's go look at the gardens." She must have looked a little startled, for he continued quickly. "They're famous, you know, and they're at their loveliest in the moonlight."

She put down her cup and saucer, accepted his hand and smiled up at him. "I'd like to see them very much."

CHAPTER FIVE

A bright harvest moon hung low and full in the sky, touching the house and gardens with a milky light, illuminating the oyster-shell paths that wound among the rosebushes and silvering the glass-rimmed top of the old tower. The sweet scent of honeysuckle mingled with the rich, loamy odor of freshly turned earth and the heady smell of red roses.

Devereaux House stood on the crest of the hill, facing the river. The ground, thick with pines, fell away toward the water's edge. The only break in the evergreens was the curving avenue of live oaks that marked the driveway.

The tower rose to the west of the house at the highest point of the hill. Leah recalled from the guidebook that an early-day bride had had the tower built so she could watch for the return of her husband's ship.

As Leah and Merrick walked along the length of the west veranda, she realized that the two-story verandas circled the house and that screen doors gave easy access to them from each room. She and Merrick went down the central steps and entered the garden.

Yew hedges shaped in triangles and squares formed an intricate pattern around the base of the tower. Oyster shells crunched beneath Leah and Merrick's feet. A nightingale trilled its melody, each note clear and liquid and perfect. The air still held the heat of the day, but a shimmering breeze swept cooler air up from the river; with it came the smell of water and pine and something darker, heavier: a musky scent of age, old wood, old earth.

Leah wondered how many mistresses of Devereaux House had walked along this path in years past. Was it from this tower that Marthe had waited for Timothy? Had she kept a pistol hidden in the folds of her skirt?

Leah shivered.

Merrick noticed at once. "Let's go back. I'll shield you from the wind."

She hesitated, drawn by the tower. "Can we go up in it?" she asked impulsively.

"What?"

"The tower. Let's go up. It must have a marvelous view." She moved ahead of him, turning toward the tower door. Then she saw the chain and stopped.

Merrick caught up with her. "I keep forgetting that you don't know us, that everything is new to you. The tower door's been locked and chained for years. I've forgotten why. Rotten flooring or unsteady stairs, something dangerous. Cissy wanted to have the whole thing pulled down five or six years ago, but Aunt Carrie wired back from Nice to let it stand. It was built by a local architect of some renown."

Leah stared up at the glass windows at the top. The tower was even more intriguing close up. "Look at the funny sides," she exclaimed.

"It's built in an octagonal shape," Merrick explained.

"It would be fun just to peek inside."

Merrick laughed. "You and Kent Ellis. He was asking about keys just the other day, but even the keys are long gone. We'd have to take a hacksaw to those chains to get in."

"Who's Kent Ellis?"

"You'll meet him one of these days. He's a protege of Aunt Carrie's, and he's doing some digging near the old slave quarters."

"What in the world for?"

"Oh, he's an archaeologist. He's on the staff at Mefford Junior College, and he's nutty about everything old. I mean really old. He's digging up some refuse deposits and reopening a well. He's especially interested in the area where the overseer's house once stood. Aunt Carrie's fascinated by all of it, and she's let him pitch a tent on the far side of the hill, near the old slave cabins." There was a note of reserve in Merrick's voice.

"Don't you like him?" A bold question, but she felt comfortable in asking Merrick. She would never have asked Cissy or John Edward.

He shrugged. "I have no reason not to like him. It's just . . ." He paused, then said openly, "All right, I'll tell you what bothers me. Three things happened here this summer. Aunt Carrie came home from Nice. Kent Ellis cozied himself into the family circle. And The Whispering Lady reappeared after an absence of nineteen years."

They walked on past the tower, down a curving path that led into the heart of the garden. Azaleas swept like open arms along the periphery. Weeping willows, their long slender fronds swaying in the night breeze, encircled a huge pond. Leah smelled the sweetness of jasmine, honeysuckle and oleander, but her mind was on The Whispering Lady. The magazine article said she had been seen again in the Devereaux gardens. Now Merrick lumped the ghost's reappearance with Carrie Devereaux's return and Kent Ellis's arrival.

"Where is she seen?" Leah asked, and her throat felt tight.

"There." Merrick pointed at the pond and its rustling guard of willows. "Across that footbridge. Can you see the gazebo?"

A graceful summerhouse loomed ahead, darker than the shadows. So that was where a ghost moved in the deep of night. And if a ghost walked again, there was evil, Louisa had written. Evil, growing and spreading, reaching out to touch them all.

"I don't believe in ghosts."

"Neither do I," Merrick replied, but his voice had an odd sound to it.

She looked at him sharply. "You have some idea about it, don't you?"

He was silent for a long moment. Then, finally, he said, "No. No, not really."

She experienced a twinge of disappointment. She had felt so close to him all evening—until now, when he'd made such a careful, noncommittal response. He knew or suspected something about the ghostly appearances. She was certain of it. But he wasn't going to share his thoughts with her.

"Come on, Leah, let's walk down to the dock." Once again, his voice was warm.

He took her hand and guided her along the path. She asked him about the river, its depth and currents, and was glad that she managed to keep her voice relaxed and casual. Her heart was beating with excitement and something more, an incredible awareness of his nearness.

They reached the dock, which looked rickety and worn. Leah stepped out onto the weathered boards and looked out at the dark water, now a curving band of silver in the moonlight. As she trod on an uneven board, she twisted her ankle and began to fall.

Merrick reached out to catch her, and then she was in his arms. She looked up, but the moon was behind him and she couldn't see his face clearly. Her heart thudded wildly. She had an instant's sense of the rightness of being in his arms, but at almost the same moment, they broke apart.

"Are you all right?" he asked. She wondered if she heard a hint of breathlessness in his voice, but perhaps that was only her own feeling.

"I'm fine. Thanks for helping me." She looked around at the dark pockets of shadows beneath the willows. "So this is where The Whispering Lady appears. How many times has she been seen this summer?"

"Three, I think." There was a note of reserve in his voice again.

"Has anything bad happened to Grandmother?"

He stiffened beside her. "Why do you ask?"

"She told me about her accidents when The Whispering Lady was seen . . . and my parents were lost."

"Oh. So she told you that."

Suddenly, Leah felt shut out, pushed away. Why didn't he want to talk about the danger to Carrie?

They stood there for a few moments, neither of them speaking. Then Leah started over the wooden bridge. "I'd better go in now."

"I'll walk with you." His voice was still slightly aloof. But when they had reached the house, he put his hand on her arm. "I'll take you around tomorrow, to see the plantations."

Then he turned away and was gone in the night.

A long moment passed before she walked up the back steps. Once inside the house, she hesitated, then returned to the library.

Cissy looked up and studied her intently.

Leah smiled. "Now I've seen the Devereaux gardens by moonlight, and I found them to be lovely. I've just come in to say good night. And, Grandmother, I'm so happy to be here."

Carrie Devereaux's dark eyes sparkled. "You can't know, child, what it means to us to have you here." She began to struggle up out of her chair.

"Don't get up," Leah said quickly.

"I want to go upstairs with you."

Leah helped her to rise, and they walked slowly out of the drawing room, Leah holding her grandmother's arm to support her. It was odd, she thought, how quickly and easily she'd come to think of calling Carrie Grandmother, the name that for so long had belonged to Louisa. But it came naturally, and she knew she was going to love this grandmother, too, hard and prickly though Carrie Devereaux could be. Leah felt certain she could bring happiness to her and ease some of the sorrow that still lay in her eyes.

They took their time climbing the curving central stairs, stopping twice for Carrie to rest.

"Tomorrow we'll show you all of Devereaux Plantation, and you can see the gardens in the early morning. They are so lovely when the mists rise. That's the time to imagine what it was like when Claude Devereaux first built here."

They stopped in front of the bedroom to which Henry had brought Leah in the afternoon.

Carrie Devereaux looked up at her sternly. "It took great courage, child, to come into a wild land and struggle to build a home."

"I'm sure it did."

Leah's grandmother thumped her cane. "We Devereaux have courage. You remember that." Then she reached out, gently touched the ornate doorknob and opened the door. "I've not stood here for more than twenty years. This was my daughter's room." She took a deep breath. "And now it will be yours. Good night, child."

Leah stood in the open doorway as her grandmother slowly made her way down the hall. Then she went inside and closed the door behind her.

A single lamp burned softly on the dressing table. The bedcovers had been turned down, revealing pale yellow sheets. A pitcher of ice water sat on the table by the bed, along with a cut-glass tumbler. The pale gray walls with their rose pattern seemed as muted as a seascape at dawn.

Suddenly Leah had a vision of another room, a cheerful girl's room in faraway Rockport, filled with modern white furniture, bright travel posters and a bulletin board thick with pictures, notes and all the happy memorabilia of her school years. She looked slowly around the elegant bedroom in which she stood, and had a sudden suffocating sense of what it would be like to grow up at Devereaux Plantation.

Her nightgown lay across the pillows. Her hairbrush and comb were in place on the dressing table. She walked forward and watched her image in the mirror. She leaned close and stared into her eyes and thought of the portrait in the dining room. Her eyes. Her mother's eyes. Dark pools in a narrow, pale face.

Leah whirled away from the mirror, but she couldn't escape her mother, not in this room suddenly laden with her memory. She faced the mirror again. She wasn't Mary Ellen. Dark eyes stared back at her.

She was Leah Devereaux Shaw—and didn't she owe something to the shadowy figures who had been her parents? And to her newly found grandmother?

Leah nodded slowly.

So she wouldn't let fear or the hint of horrors long hidden drive her away. She would face down John Edward's enmity and Cissy's limp welcome.

She would not even let Merrick's charm dissuade her from finding out about the ghost who was again walking in the Devereaux gardens.

She undressed and put on her nightgown, then looked for a long moment at the old-fashioned bed, which her mother had used as a girl. Determinedly, she climbed into it and lay there watching moonlit patterns on the walls for a seemingly endless time.

CHAPTER SIX

Leah woke up as the first streaks of dawn pearled the eastern sky. She got out of bed, pushed open the screen door and stepped onto the veranda to look out across the gardens, dimly seen now in the early-morning mist, the pinks and reds and yellows of the roses barely visible. How utterly lovely—and Merrick would be coming to take her to see the plantations today. A tingle of excitement pulsed within her. She was so eager to see him. Then she remembered how he had withdrawn last night when she'd asked about the accidents that had threatened Carrie.

Did he think that she threatened her grandmother?

It was an ugly thought. But ugly things had happened at Devereaux Plantation. Surely he didn't suspect her of being part of any plot. He was wary about the archaeologist, Kent Ellis. Perhaps she should make it a point to talk to Kent Ellis as soon as possible. And she wanted to find out more about the night her mother and father had left on the yacht—and more, much more, about her mother. Her grandmother had said Old Jason loved her mother. If he was still alive, she would talk to him.

She walked to the end of the veranda. From there she could see the pier where The New Star had anchored and the octagonal tower high on the bluff overlooking the river.

Later, Leah would wonder what impulse drove her to return to her room and hurry, pulling on a blue cotton blouse, white shorts and sneakers. She brushed her hair and added a touch of lipstick, then slipped out into the hall and down the stairs.

The house lay silent. Only the frenzied, cheerful chirp of the birds broke the early-morning quiet. Once outside the house, she stood at the top of the garden, looking down toward the small pond and the summerhouse. She had almost started down the path to the summerhouse when she heard the sound of footsteps on the crushed oyster shells. She swung around.

Cissy moved purposefully, her hands swinging at her sides, her eyes on the path. When she looked up, only a few feet from Leah, her hand flew up to her throat.

"I'm sorry," Leah said quickly. "I've startled you."

Cissy drew her breath in sharply. "Not at all. I see you are an early riser, too. I often walk at this hour. It's so peaceful, so lovely."

The sun was beginning its rise now. A pale pink-and-orange light touched the tops of the tall trees and the glassed-in tower. Leah thought it would be glorious to see the river and the house now from the tower.

Impulsively, she reached out and touched Cissy's arm. "Could we go up in the tower? Merrick says he doesn't even know if there are any keys left. But didn't you close it up? Surely there are keys somewhere—"

The arm beneath her hand went rigid, and she drew away.

Cissy's face flamed. "Didn't he tell you? The tower is unsafe. It's dreadfully dangerous. I keep telling Aunt Carrie it must be pulled down." Then she quieted her breathing and managed a smile. "You mustn't listen to anyone who suggests entering it." She took Leah by the elbow. "Come, now, I'm not being a good hostess—" She broke off abruptly and laughed. "There I go, forgetting that I needn't feel responsible anymore. But Aunt Carrie was gone for so long that I got used to taking care of everything. Still, I'll stand in for her this morning and insist we go in and have breakfast."

Leah gave one last look at the tower, then followed Cissy up the steps to the second-floor veranda and a breakfast table with a commanding view of the garden.

Hal pushed back his chair and rose to greet her. "Morning, Leah."

"Good morning."

As Cissy sat down beside her husband, Leah noticed how her hand touched his shoulder. It was the touch of a woman who cared, deeply and passionately. Cissy obviously adored her slender, aristocratic and, to Leah, somewhat boring husband.

After she sat down in the wicker chair and accepted a cup of coffee from Henry, she felt a moment's amusement. How odd life was. Perhaps she had been naive to assume that because Cissy seemed selfish and preoccupied with her social status, she wasn't capable of love. Leah had been wrong about that.

Cissy now appeared friendlier, more relaxed. "How long can you stay with us?" she asked as she passed a basket of fresh, hot blueberry muffins.

Leah buttered a muffin, then looked up in surprise mixed with bewilderment. "Do you know, I hadn't even thought about that. I work at a travel agency in Dallas. When Louisa died, I went home, of course, to take care of everything." She didn't want to talk about finding that just-begun letter and the magazine article. "Then I decided to try and find out more about what happened to my parents, so I called my boss and asked for two more weeks. So I suppose . . ."

"Don't be absurd."

A man's deep voice seemed to fill the veranda. Leah turned in her chair and saw Merrick approaching.

"You can call him today and tell him that you won't be coming back. You're home now."

Home.

The sunlight flooded around him, much as it had yesterday afternoon when she'd first seen him. Again he was in command, his voice resonant, his expression full of warmth. There was no indication that last night he had seemed aloof, even for a moment. He reached out and touched her shoulder.

His arrival considerably brightened her morning. Breakfast was no longer a mundane, necessary activity. It was fun, and everything tasted like the ambrosia of the gods.

Finally, Merrick waved Henry away. "Enough food, enough coffee. Our newest member of the family has much to see today."

"Where are you going?" Cissy asked.

"We'll start with the house. Then I want to take Leah to see all the plantations." To Leah, he explained, "We have five, and I especially want you to see Ashwood, where I live. But first, a guided tour of Devereaux House."

He pulled her to her feet and held her hand a little longer than was necessary. Then he gave it a firm squeeze and led the way downstairs.

In giving her a guided tour of the house, Merrick recounted stories about the former inhabitants. As much as she loved the house and the stories, which gave her a sense of community with long-lost kin, she loved being with Merrick. She loved the eagerness in his eyes when he talked and the way his hair flamed like copper in the morning sun. She loved the feel of his hand on her arm and the deep sound of his voice. And she wondered if he felt at all as she did.

Her uncertainty made her voice brisk. "I've enjoyed seeing the house with you, but I don't want to keep you from your work."

"I'm taking the day off. Today is going to be all yours. I want to show you everything you'd like to see."

Leah hesitated, then asked, "Will you show me where The New Star was?"

For an instant, the pleasure left his face; then he nodded.

They went outside and headed down the avenue of trees. The Mefford River glittered in the sunlight. About fifty yards from the water, they came to the point where the country road intersected the treelined avenue. Yesterday—could it only have been yesterday?—John Edward's Porsche had angled across the road, blocking Leah's access to the house.

She said it aloud without thinking. "John Edward didn't want me to see Grandmother."

Merrick frowned. "I don't know, Leah. That might not be true."

"I don't think there can be any doubt about it," she countered.

Merrick was looking at her strangely. "You have to remember how much you look like Mary Ellen."

She stared at him, puzzled. "What does that have to do with it?"

He took her hand and held it in a firm, strong grip. "Your mother was supposed to marry John Edward."

"John Edward!" she exclaimed. Carrie hadn't told her that. Oh, how awful it must have been—the wedding planned, the dress bought, the guests invited, and her mother, driven to desperation, running to the man she truly loved.

"Carrie didn't tell you?"

"No. It must have been dreadful."

"It was. I was just a little kid then, but I remember it like yesterday."

"But why in the world would Grandmother want her daughter to marry him?"

"The pride of the Devereaux." Merrick's voice was grim now.

They had reached the dock, and the sound of their footsteps on the wooden planks hung in the still air.

"Yes, the pride of the Devereaux." He shaded his eyes against the sun. "I don't know if you can ever quite understand what it means to Carrie to be a Devereaux, to carry on the family name. That's why she never likes it to be mentioned that we were really Simpsons, born to my mother before she married Andrew Devereaux. We are Aunt Carrie's avenue to the future, to the continuation of the Devereaux name. And, of course, it seemed quite reasonable to her that your mother would marry John Edward. It would work out, because, of course, they weren't really blood kin, but he carried the Devereaux name. And you have to understand that they liked each other. In fact, I think he loved her, because he's never married. Yes, it was a terrible shock to everyone. That's why Carrie wouldn't have a thing to do with her daughter after she ran away."

"Carrie must have been very angry."

"She was. And she felt sorry for John Edward." He looked at Leah, than said slowly, "When he sees you, it must hurt like the devil."

"Surely not after all these years!"

"Can you ever really forget someone you've loved?" he asked quietly.

They walked on in silence, and Leah realized they were almost at the end of the rickety wooden dock where the yacht had tied up. She shaded her eyes against the brilliant morning sun.

It hadn't been sunny that day when her mother and father had walked on the weathered dock for the last time.

Leah shivered.

Merrick slipped his arm around her shoulders. "Don't, Leah. It doesn't do any good to imagine."

He understood. She clung to that. Merrick knew how she felt inside.

"I don't remember them," she said huskily. She looked up at him, still secure in the shelter of his arm. "You knew them. Oh, Merrick, what were they like?"

He hesitated, then said slowly, "I was just a kid, as I said. And that day was the only time I ever met your father."

She waited tensely to hear more.

"He was furious. Your mother was mad, too. She was quick to get mad, but just as quick to have it blow over, like a spring storm. And she laughed a lot. I remember that." He looked down at Leah and smiled. "It's been so long ago now. But I always remember that she laughed a lot."

Leah pictured a dark-haired girl standing on the dock, the river breeze blowing her soft white dress. The girl looked over her shoulder, and her face curved with laughter. Sudden tears burned in Leah's eyes.

Merrick pulled her close. "Don't cry. I'm here, and it's all right. Whatever happened, it's all right."

She wanted to object, to say that it wasn't all right, that the truth about her parents could make a difference. But suddenly his mouth was on hers, and there was no more time for thought, only for feeling, for the sweep of happiness that lifted her like a current of air carrying a bird into the heavens.

When they did speak, in soft and jumbled phrases, Leah didn't try to make sense of what was happening, didn't try to measure and weigh it. She only knew she'd never felt this way before.

"I had no idea it could be true," Merrick murmured.

"What could be true?"

"Love at first sight."

She tried to shake her head, but his mouth found hers again. And again. Then, because her heart was beating too fast, and because warmth and a wonderful desire flooded her, she pulled away. "We'd . . . we'd better go in."

He held her tightly. "Do you really want to?"

She looked up at him, her eyes vulnerable.

"All right," he said with a hint of laughter in his voice. "I'll take you in, Miss Leah. But I want you to know the battle lines are drawn. You're going to be mine. You've come home to Devereaux Plantation, and you're never going to leave."

She tugged at his hand, and they started back up the wide, oak-lined avenue.

"Never?" she asked, bantering, trying to ease the pounding of her heart.

"Never."

As they neared Devereaux House, Leah looked at it with new eyes. Would she never leave it? Had Merrick meant that literally? Before she thought, she asked impulsively, "But, Merrick, didn't you say you lived at Ashwood?"

"Yes," he replied easily. "But it isn't far from here. Actually, Cissy and Hal have lived here for years, all during the time Aunt Carrie was in Nice. And, of course, she's had them stay on because it really is their home. She wouldn't put them out."

"Of course not."

"And John Edward's always lived here, too."

"What does he do?"

"He's a lawyer, and you know I'm a farmer. But today I'm your tour guide."

After they lunched on the west veranda with Carrie, Merrick took Leah on a leisurely tour of Mefford. When they stood on the bluff and looked down at the old wharf, she said, "I feel like I've come home."

He slipped an arm around her shoulders. "You have. Just like all your forebears who sailed into this harbor. The only difference is that you came by way of a Vega."

She laughed; "That's quite a difference." She shaded her eyes to look out at the brownish river. "It looks deep."

"It is. Either swim well or wear water wings if you fall into the Mefford. But it's the reason the town is one of the finest natural draft harbors on the coast. Settlers first landed in 1711. They built their homes up here. Then there was the fire."

"A bad one?"

"Very." He pointed toward the old frame homes behind them. "Of those early houses, only that gold-toned one, the third house, survived the fire. It's the oldest house still standing in Mefford."

Leah stared at him with admiration. "My goodness, you do know your town!"

A look of surprise touched his face. "You know, I suppose I do. Guess I had too many third-grade tours with a teacher who was a history nut. But it does make it fun. I suppose I know something about every house and every family in this old part of town."

Then they took a walk through the cemetery. Today, with Merrick by her side, it wasn't depressing or frightening. Leah gave only a glance to the stone shaped like a sailing sloop. Instead, she moved from stone to stone and listened as he told her about some early renegade-type Devereaux.

"So not all my ancestors have been predictable," she observed.

"Not at all." He laughed. "Actually, I learned about them from Old Jason. Aunt Carrie would be appalled if she knew."

Hand in hand, they walked back up the brick path toward the street.

"I'll have to admit, I've been feeling rather daunted by this grand family," Leah said. "Now I feel much more at home."

"As a Devereaux in name only, I can well understand that," he agreed. "Old Jason never tired of telling us Devereaux stories." His voice had softened when he mentioned Jason.

She squeezed his hand. "You really cared for him, didn't you?"

"Oh, yes. And I still do."

"Still do?" An understanding flooded her, she held tightly to his hand. "Is he still alive?"

"Yes, and he claims to be a hundred and three. That may be so. His memory stretches back for generations. A lot of those memories of his youth are clearer to him than what happened yesterday."

"I want to see him. Oh, Merrick, I want so much to talk to him! He knew my mother—better than anyone. Please, take me to him—now!"

They couldn't go fast enough to suit her. She tugged at his elbow and set almost a running pace along the two blocks to the car. Once in the station wagon, she sat on the edge of the seat, impatient as they stopped for red lights, eager when they reached the highway. When the car jolted down a sandy track that led onto Devereaux Plantation, she said happily, "He cared for my mother, didn't he?"

"If ever Old Jason cared for anyone, it was Mary Ellen, though he was wonderful to all of us. But she held a special place in his heart. And, since I've met you, I understand why."

"Do you think I'm so much like her?"

"Very much."

They passed a tumbledown heap of old buildings. Merrick said, "That's one of the places where Ellis is excavating. Next time we'll stop and take a look."

The car rattled over a wooden bridge and slowed to a stop in front of a weathered cabin. An old wagon wheel marked the edge of the drive. As Merrick opened the car door for her, she stumbled a little in her eagerness, then started ahead of him up the hard-packed dirt path.

The front door of the cabin swung open, and, a very old man stepped out, shading his eyes against the sunlight. He was frail and thin, his shoulders stooped, his dark hair grizzled.

"Old Jason," Leah called out.

His head jerked back. He raised his hands out in front of him, as if warding off an attack. "Oh, dear Lord." His voice rose in a wail. "It's Miss Mary Ellen. She done come for me—and I know it's my time. Miss Mary Ellen, I didn't mean to do no bad thing—" He fell to the ground and lay there in a faint.

Leah knelt beside him while Merrick went inside the cabin to call for help. Until the ambulance arrived, she stayed with Jason, holding his hand and, when he opened his eyes, explaining that she was Mary Ellen's daughter.

Jason was embarrassed then. "I'm a silly old fool," he gasped.

"No, oh, no, Old Jason. I know you were my mother's best friend and Merrick's. Please, now, please get well, and then you and I can talk about my mother when she was little."

He clung to her hand, his own weak and dry. "I do like to remember that. I do like to remember, before the bad times came. . . ." Then he closed his eyes.

"Jason?"

"It's all right." Merrick reassured her. "He's just resting."

"Resting. Mighty tired, I am."

Leah didn't cry until after the ambulance had taken Jason away.

Merrick gave her a little shake. "Leah, don't be so upset. He just fainted. He'll rest up in the hospital and be all right—or at least as fine as a man his age can be."

"I thought I made him have a heart attack." She wiped a hand against her tear-streaked face.

"No. He's unsteady on his feet and prone to fainting spells, that's all. Why, he didn't even want to go to the hospital, but I'd told Dr. Jarvis to give him a private room and baby him for a few days. When he's stronger, he'll talk to you."

Leah felt better by the time they reached the plantation house. She grasped Merrick's hand. "It was a wonderful day until—"

"Go rest, and don't worry about Old Jason. I promise you, he will be fine."

His voice was confident, of course. He was always confident, but his sense of surety refreshed her.

"Thank you, then, for a wonderful day."

"I'll see you at dinner."

Once she was inside the house, her feeling of happiness ebbed as she thought about Old Jason. She stopped by her grandmother's room to tell her what had happened.

Carrie was sitting in a petit-point-covered chair by the window, holding an unopened book in her lap. She looked up with a smile when Leah entered. Upon hearing the story, the old lady shook her head, but she was still smiling.

"He is an old fool—has the vapors like that. But he'll be fine. I'll have Lilac send him some special beef broth. Now, don't you fret, child. He will be fine, and it will mean the world to him to have you here." She reached out and took Leah's hand. "Did you have a happy afternoon, my dear?"

"Oh, Grandmother, yes. We had so much fun."

She thought about the afternoon, the good part of it, as she walked down the hall to her room. She was startled when she looked at her watch and saw the time. It was almost six. She and Merrick had made a day of it. What would they do tomorrow?

The idea of a tomorrow spent with him lifted the last edges of her depression. There would be a happy tomorrow, and many more. Jason would get well, and she would talk to him and find out more about her mother. She could learn so much—Then the dark remembrance came. Could she learn what had happened to her mother and father on the last night of their lives?

But tonight she wouldn't worry about that. Tonight she would not let the mystery of their death ruin the lovely yet tenuous bond between her and Merrick.

After her bath, a languorous one, she slipped into a dramatic black-and-white linen dress that emphasized the darkness of her eyes and hair.

The look in Merrick's eyes as she came down the stairs told her that she did indeed look lovely.

They went into the library for cocktails and, when the gong sounded a half hour later, walked into the dining room together. The conversation at dinner was relaxed. Cissy recounted the latest news of the Mefford Historical Society. Hal discussed a hunt that was planned for next week. John Edward regaled them with the details of his day in court. Carrie listened to everyone and made occasional dry comments.

But when they went back to the library after dinner, the atmosphere was changed. Leah felt as if she were in a room full of mannequins, not people—and she knew why. Tonight they would talk about the long-ago evening when The New Star left Devereaux Plantation.

Her grandmother took her place in the wing chair that made her look frail and small. Cissy and Hal sat side by side on a petit-point love seat. Merrick leaned against the mantel, his eyes fastened on Leah. John Edward stood also, his legs apart, his hands jammed in his pockets.

Each face, as it turned toward Carrie Devereaux, was smooth and blank. Even, Leah realized with a pang, Merrick's face. And what did this evening mean to John Edward, who at one time had hoped to marry her mother? How did he feel? Did he still care for the memory of Mary Ellen, or did he hate the woman who had jilted him?

Carrie Devereaux looked from one to the other. "All of you were here the afternoon Mary Ellen came."

Hal shifted on the love seat. "Now, Aunt Carrie, you remember that was before Cissy and I had decided to marry. We were just going around together then. I'd dropped by to see her, but I didn't stay to meet Mary Ellen and the new husband. Seemed to me like it might be awkward, so I begged off. Told Cissy I'd better get home and see if the shutters were going up all right. That was the day before the big blow."

No one commented. Leah supposed it seemed natural to all of them that Hal made it a point to avoid any unpleasantness. Cissy certainly looked as if this were a perfectly natural way to behave. It was clear that whatever Hal did would be absolutely all right with Cissy. Was it physical passion that attracted her, or Hal's social position? Cissy was obsessed with pride of place, but she also seemed genuinely obsessed with Hal. She must have been irritated when Mary Ellen's arrival drove away the beau she so definitely wanted.

"The wind was rising when I left," Hal continued. "Everybody was boarding up."

"That's what I was doing," John Edward chimed in. "I was helping Jason with the shutters when The New Star came into view." He shook his head, and Leah could picture his bewilderment of nineteen years ago. "I couldn't believe it at first. But Old Jason knew."

Carrie nodded calmly enough, but her hands twisted her fine cambric handkerchief into a knot.

"Old Jason's face was as gray as the sky," John Edward went on. "He said, 'I don't know how I'm gain' to tell Miss Mary Ellen.'"

"I saw the boat arrive," Merrick offered. "I was boarding up the third-floor windows. I ran down to the pier to help them tie up. I was there when Old Jason told Mary Ellen that Aunt Carrie had left."

"Tom wanted to pull right out," John Edward said. "He was furious. He stood there on the pier, the wind flattening his clothes against him, and he looked ready to fight. God, the wind was bad. The palmettos sounded like cane being thrashed. But Mary Ellen said she wasn't leaving until she knew what Old Jason meant about The Whispering Lady—and her mother's accidents."

Merrick nodded. "She stormed off up the path. That's the last I saw of her. The wind was blowing harder and harder. I went back to help batten down the rest of the house."

"Yeah," John Edward said slowly, "she was mad as hell."

"Why?" Leah asked.

For an instant, John Edward's eyes focused on her. "God, you do look like Mary Ellen." Then his mouth thinned. "But you aren't really like her. She was a hellcat when she was crossed."

Leah shrank a little. Her parents were so indistinct to her. Louisa Shaw had rarely spoken of them. Perhaps she had felt that if she did it would open the floodgates, and she would have to tell all.

But as John Edward described it, the reunion on the pier was awkward. Tom, furious that Mary Ellen's mother left, had wanted to sail away immediately.

Leah saw him a little more clearly, young and full of pride.

"They had a hell of a fight, right there on the pier," John Edward said. He recalled it with a kind of relish. "Mary Ellen was raging—at me, at her mother, at Tom. Then she said she didn't care what kind of stiff-necked, self-centered fool her mother was, she didn't intend to leave until she knew the truth about Aunt Carrie's accidents.

"Tom went back to the boat, leaving Mary Ellen and me on the pier. He didn't intend, ever, to set foot on Devereaux land again.

"It wasn't even five o'clock yet, but it was already getting dark because of the storm clouds. The sky was slate-gray with streaks of red, and the wind was gusting from the south-southeast. I told Mary Ellen all I knew while we walked up to the house. I left her on the lower veranda, looking down toward the pond and the willows—that's where the ghost's always seen. I went on upstairs to help Jason board the windows. No one knew how bad the storm was going to be. I had so much to do that I didn't even think about her until after dark, and it was raining hard by then. But when morning came, the boat was gone. I was sorry about it, but not surprised. I knew Tom wanted to get the hell out, no matter how bad the weather was."

After a moment's silence, Cissy said hesitantly, "I may have been the last person to talk to her." She frowned in recollection. "We had a glass of wine in the library. I tried to talk her into staying until Aunt Carrie came back."

"What did she say?" Carrie asked sharply.

Cissy looked uncomfortable.

"Go ahead," Carrie insisted.

Reluctantly, Cissy continued. "You have to remember that Mary Ellen was furious. As much at her husband as at you."

"What did she say?"

Cissy looked down at the diamonds sparkling on her finger. "She said you were stubborn as a goat, but not any more stubborn than she was. I knew about the scene she and Tom had on the pier. So I asked her, and maybe I shouldn't have, but I asked her what she was going to do. She said she was going to show Tom that no one could order her to do anything. Besides, she said it was too dangerous to leave with the storm coming. The last I saw of her, she was heading back down to the boat to tell him they were going to lie to." Cissy shrugged. "Actually, I thought she would prevail. You know what a strong personality she had. I also thought Tom would have better sense than to set sail in that kind of weather. It never occurred to me that they'd leave. When we found the boat gone the next morning, I couldn't believe it."

Carrie Devereaux looked incredibly old and weary. She looked around the room at each of them. "But don't you see, this leaves us where we've always been—with the boat sailing and never being seen again. We always thought it had gone down and that everyone was lost at sea. Yet now we know Leah and Louisa survived. What happened to Tom and Mary Ellen, and to The New Star? And why did Louisa run away to Texas, taking Leah with her? In her letter, she said she must have been wrong about what happened the night of the storm. For God's sake, what did happen?"

Her plea hung in the air. No one moved or spoke, but to Leah, the atmosphere of strain in the library was plainly evident. She saw it in the chalky white of Cissy's face, in the studied emptiness of John Edward's eyes, in the tautness of Merrick's hunched shoulders. They'd all been here that night. Did one of them know more than he was willing to admit?

John Edward spoke finally. "The next morning..." He paused and swallowed. "I don't know if this has anything to do with it, but the next morning when I came down to the library, I noticed something funny." He glanced at the east wall, and everyone else did, too. "Do you remember the silver dueling pistols that hung there among the other guns?"

Carrie Devereaux nodded slowly.

"They were gone."

CHAPTER SEVEN

Leah lay sleepless in the four-poster, staring with unseeing eyes at the pattern of moonlight against the wall. Images whirled in her mind. She saw a slate-gray sky and trees bending beneath the wind; a slender, angry young woman storming up a hill toward a house that had once been her home—and a set of dueling pistols hanging against the library wall.

She moved restlessly. What did it all mean? She didn't know, but she remembered that years ago she'd opened a sealed cistern behind their house in Rockport. Dead, sour air had choked her. There were things better kept closed.

Did she really want to find out what had happened that storm-ridden night?

Dreadful visions moved in her mind. She thought of Marthe, who'd killed her lover. She remembered her mother's face in the portrait in the dining room. Mary Ellen's face, now smiling, now angry, came together and apart, like broken pieces of a puzzle.

Only one tiny fact stood between Leah and her visions. Louisa Shaw had said in her letter that an evil existed at Devereaux Plantation. Leah felt that that evil was near, threatening her, threatening her grandmother. She slept finally, but in her dreams the wind moaned and thunder crashed, trees split and cracked, and horror lurked just out of sight.

NEAR MIDNIGHT, SATURDAY, MAY 9,1863

The door creaked, ever so slowly. Marthe lay rigid, yet she forced herself to breathe evenly. Oh, God, it must be Randolph! Did he suspect? The door began to open. Her fingernails jabbed into her palms. If he came in, if he pulled back the covers and found her lying in bed, fully dressed . . . Through barely slitted eyes she saw his large form, a darkness against the open doorway. Could he see the rise and fall of the bedcovers as she breathed? Finally, very slowly, the door closed. Marthe still lay rigid. He might come back. And what if he waited out in the hall by her door? She licked her lips in fear. She would leave by the door to the veranda.Randolph was so hateful, his breath thick with whiskey, his eyes red-rimmed and angry. Last night he had found her in the garden and twisted her arm until it ached, warning her that he would see her in hell before he would ever let her be with Timothy again. Oh, Timothy, she thought. She loved him so. Was he coming? Was he even now crossing the river? Abruptly, she threw back the covers and swung her legs over the side of the bed. The tiny chimes of her Dresden clock sou nded . . . ten . . . eleven . . . twelve. It wouldn't be long now!

Leah awoke with a start, heart thudding erratically. She raised herself up and listened. Then she heard a dog's shrill, frenzied yelping and knew that was what had awakened her. The yelp sounded again. The dog must be in trouble. She got out of bed and hurried toward the open back windows that overlooked the garden. All she saw were the dark contours of the garden and the glint of moonlight on the pond.

The yelp came again, then was abruptly cut off in mid-cry. Leah frowned. Something was hurting the dog. She picked up her dressing gown and slipped it on. After stepping into her slippers, she hurried out the screen door and ran to the porch railing.

From above, the palmetto palms looked oddly stunted, but the pine trees that rimmed the garden were huge, dark triangles against the night sky. The stars shone brilliantly. The octagonal tower loomed to her left, appearing almost sinister. The oyster-shell paths were clearly visible in the moonlight.

She thought the dog must be somewhere in the garden or beyond. But now it was absolutely quiet.

Leah ran lightly down the veranda to the central steps, her slippers slapping against the wooden treads. At the base of the stairs, she paused again to listen. The night air was chilly, damp from the river. She shivered and drew her dressing gown closer. Something moved on the far side of the pond, and she clearly heard a crackling of twigs.

Then, to her horror, she saw a luminous whiteness out there, perhaps the size of a person. It seemed to be coming nearer to the edge of the pond. It made several jerky movements, almost as if in a curtsy, before it began to back slowly away. As it went deeper into the shadows of the weeping willows, it disappeared.

Leah stood frozen at the top of the garden. The silence around her was as unmoving and leaden as a funeral pall. She had seen . . . what had she seen? Something frightful, something touched with doom, and it held her rigid with fear.

Go and see, she told herself.

Her hands and legs trembled.

She didn't believe in ghosts. But something had moved, something luminous and flowing, in a jerky, inhuman way. Leah's mouth tightened. Something had moved, and she would bet her last cent that somebody had moved it. Anger pumped through her. Abruptly, she started down the path to the pond. She would go and see what was there.

Then her steps slowed. Louisa had written that if a ghost walked again in the garden, it meant there was evil at Devereaux Plantation. But evil implied human will and decision, a human agency.

Leah continued to walk forward, but now every one of her senses was alert and wary. She stopped when she reached the narrow, low-railed bridge that arched over the pond. It was very dark on the other side, the willow trees thick as hummocky grass. And somewhere beneath their hanging tendrils, that luminous whiteness had disappeared.

Leah stepped out onto the bridge. Her feet slipped a little on the dew-wet wooden boards. Midway across, she stopped again. She didn't know what had made her stop. Maybe she'd heard a rustle in the undergrowth. Or was it more atavistic than that?

Nevertheless, she knew with absolute certainty that she shouldn't cross the bridge and step into the black shadows beyond. She stared at the silent clump of willows, their long, slender fronds hanging like witches' hair, dark and impenetrable. Like wildfire racing up a tinder-dry tree, panic consumed her.

She whirled and ran, slipping on the slick wood. The oyster shell tore her flimsy slippers, but her pace didn't slacken—not for pain or thought, not for anything. Fear rode her shoulder, whipping her to run faster still.

She reached the house and thudded up the wide, shallow steps to the first veranda, breathless now, her lungs straining for air. Stumbling, scarcely able to see, she made it up the second flight and crumpled at the top. She couldn't run another step. She huddled there, her breath coming in tortured gasps, and twisted around to look down into the garden.

Nothing moved. No sound broke the stillness. No one followed her. Yet when she looked at the moonlit pond and the dark willows beyond, she couldn't stop herself from shuddering.

Gradually, her lungs ceased to ache. She continued to stare through the balusters, but the garden remained quiet and empty.

She wasn't fooled, though. She had come close to death, had felt it with an unshakable certainty. Death had waited for her across the pond, lurking in the shadows of the willow trees.

Louisa had been right. Evil underlay Devereaux Plantation, hidden like dry rot beneath a smooth and shining surface. If Leah had gone forward, she would have known the human agency that moved behind its luminous whiteness. Did she want to know who it had been?

Another ugly question forced itself into her mind: Did she want to know what had really happened to her mother and father?

Leah shivered. Her damp gown clung to her. Stiffly, she pulled herself to her feet and walked to her room. Once she was safely inside, she latched the screen door, closed and locked the inner door, then put a straight chair beneath the door to the hall.

She didn't fear that a ghost might follow her inside. The danger she sensed was too concrete for that.

Leah woke up early to a bar of sunlight slanting across her bed and to the sound of cardinals chattering outside a window. She glanced at the bedside clock. Not quite six o'clock. No one else would be up.

She rose and dressed, putting on dark blue slacks, a yellow cotton pullover and sneakers. As she had thought, the house was still asleep when she stepped out onto the veranda. She walked to the end and looked out across the garden. In the moonlight, the shrubs had been clumps of darkness. Now they were bright sweeps of greenery, following the slope of the garden and serving as a counterpoint to the multicolored rose beds.

An occasional stone bench, its underside coated with moss, sat alongside the oyster-shell paths. The willows fringing the pond looked delicate in the softness of the early sun. A gentle breeze rippled the pond water.

All was lovely, peaceful, serene. Standing there, Leah found it hard to believe she'd run for fear of her life the night before.

Her sneakers made scarcely any sound on the shell path. This time she didn't hesitate at the bridge but crossed it decisively. She moved deep into the willows, pushing aside the dangling branches. The luminous white shape must have hovered just about where she was now. She turned and looked back at the house, then realized with a chill that she had been clearly visible from her position at the top of the garden.

She looked down and began to study the ground. Broken strands of willow, shreds of palmetto and scattered live oak leaves carpeted the sandy, uneven ground. She had no idea what she was looking for, but, being stubborn she continued to look. There were no footprints here, yet closer to the bridge there had been a smudged footprint. Leah knew that meant nothing.

She was almost ready to give it up. She could have sworn that what she'd seen had been right about here. Not far from a rustic bench . . . She was just turning away when she saw a tiny tangle of white silk clinging to the side of the bench.

Leah felt a quick thrill of triumph. There it was—proof that the ghost of Devereaux Plantation, the famous Whispering Lady, was no more ghostly than she. Ghosts didn't leave threads behind. When that inhuman shape had bowed toward her—displaying a nice touch of arrogance—the covering must have snagged against the bench.

Leah bent down and carefully pulled the little fluff of white free. This shred of silk was going to lead her to the human agency behind the ghostly appearances.

Suddenly her surge of confidence fell away. She had proof that satisfied her there was no ghost, but she didn't have anything that could link the ghost to anyone. But in her heart she felt certain that when she'd paused on the bridge last night, she hadn't been routed by a spirit of another world. Someone—someone alive—had waited in the shadows of the willows.

And she still felt certain that death had waited there, too. For her.

Then she frowned in perplexity. No, that couldn't be right. If death had waited for her, willed her to come and see, it hadn't been planned ahead of time. The danger to her would have come if the person in the willows had seized the moment to kill her. The appearance of the ghost couldn't have been planned for her benefit. No one could have known or guessed that she would hear a dog yelping in the night and go look for it.

The dog! Where was it? What—or who—had hurt it?

The ghost had been on other business last night. Frightening her was incidental. What had been the primary objective?

Presumably the ghost walked when death was near. Would death stalk someone at Devereaux Plantation today?

Leah slipped the piece of silk into her pocket and looked back the way she had come. Last night there had been no trace of the dog in the garden, and there was nothing to indicate a dog had been in this swath of greenery. She looked beyond the willows. The land began to rise past the pond. Cedars, live oaks and pine covered the hill. A faint dirt path plunged into the wooded area.

She started gingerly up the path. The pale sunlight filtered through the thick-leaved trees and twisting vines to speckle the ground beneath her feet. Once she stopped when the brush crackled to her left. A squirrel scampered up a red cedar, and she started forward again. Soon she could no longer see the willows or the pond when she looked back. There was only silent, dim wood, the trees towering nearly eighty feet above her.

The path curved sharply to the right. Just ahead, a green snake darted into the undergrowth. Leah almost turned back. She felt terribly isolated, far from any habitation. She wasn't exactly frightened, but the silence and the gloom daunted her. Then, as refreshing as a bobwhite's call, she heard the sound of someone whistling.

She came around a bend in the path and saw a man, his hands on his hips, whistling and calling for a dog. He wore Levi's, a work shirt and tan, crepe-soled boots. She liked him immediately. His dark brown hair clung to his head in soft, tight curls, and he had an equally tightly curled beard.

"Good morning," he called out, regarding her with frank and open interest. "I'm Kent Ellis, resident archaeologist, rara avis to the locals, court jester to your grandmother."

He laughed at her surprise. "Sure, I know who you are. Everybody in the county does. There hasn't been this much excitement since the organist's wife ran away with the deacon. Nobody in Mefford is talking about anything but your reappearance."

"How do they know?"

"Mrs. LeClerc's girl, Julie, told the second maid at Haverhill, who told her boyfriend, who told—"

Leah held up her hands to stem the flow of his words.

"The town's already divided on whether you're the real McCoy or an impostor. But don't worry about it. Mrs. LeClerc says you're a Devereaux, and that's better than a baptismal record."

He said it all so easily, so good-naturedly, that Leah couldn't take offense.

"I know who you are, too," she rejoined cheerfully. "It wouldn't surprise me to hear you reel off more than anyone would care to know about the Huguenots or the typical pottery found on an eighteenth-century plantation, but how in the world do you know what everybody in Mefford is saying?"

"I'm an ingratiating fellow. Besides, I'm interested in everybody. Now. Last year. Last century. Fifty thousand years ago. An academic busybody, if you want to know. And I love to show off my dig. Are you coming my way?" He gestured back up the path.

She nodded, so they walked together companionably. Twice more he interrupted a running monologue on plantation life to whistle. He was as comfortable and disarming as a front-porch rocker, which was quite a change from Devereaux Plantation. Leah hadn't realized how tense she had become until she started talking to Kent Ellis.

"Why are you so interested in Devereaux Plantation?"

"The house on the hill, honey. Always has been of interest, and I guess it always will be." He shot her a quick look. "You'll find out what it's like to be a Devereaux. Everything that happens on the plantation is of consuming interest to Mefford. Or, to be accurate, to a big part of Mefford, if not to everybody."

They broke out of the trees. Ahead of them stood a long line of slave cabins, mostly roofless, partial walls and chimneys still in place. An olive-drab tent sat near the ruins. To the left, past a grove of pines, Leah saw Jason's cabin.

"I heard you gave the old boy a shock yesterday, but the word is he's sitting up and enjoying his stay in the hospital like a maharaja, which in a way he is around here."

"Your grapevine is fast, if you've already heard about that."

Kent laughed. "Anything you want to know, just ask me."

Leah bit her lip. "I didn't mean to scare him."

"Don't worry. He's enjoying the attention. And he told the nurse, who told my girlfriend's aunt, that he wanted to see you as soon as he could. He has lots to tell you about your ma.

"Oh, I'm so glad to hear that!"

"Let's have some coffee now, and you can tell me all about yourself."

He dragged two camp chairs out of his tent and insisted on pouring coffee from his thermos into pottery mugs. The coffee tasted wonderful and reminded Leah that she hadn't breakfasted yet.

Kent told her about his excavations on Devereaux Plantation and about his companion project, oral history interviews with the oldest county residents.

"Old Jason claims he's one hundred and three. His father was a house slave, so he knows a lot about the Devereaux from the time of the Civil War on."

Their coffee finished, Kent showed Leah the excavations. He took her first to the kitchen midden behind the former overseer's cabin, pointing out the grid of heavy twine that marked the site, the three different levels and some of his findings. "They ate lots of possum and raccoon and catfish. They probably also ate a bunch of salt pork and dried beef, but those don't leave any bones."

As they walked away from the midden, he paused to whistle. "I don't know where my mutt's gone."

"Have you lost your dog?" She wondered whether or not to tell him of the yelps she'd heard the night before.

"Oh, he's not really my dog. I found him down by the river a couple of weeks ago. Somebody'd dumped him. Out-of-sight, out-of-mind murder, you know. Bill's a cute pup, about three months old, part collie and part Lab. I've been feeding him, and he likes to snuggle up to my sleeping bag at night. But he must have given up on me last night. I was really late getting back."

They walked past the overseer's cabin, and Kent looked at her hopefully. "You didn't see a puppy this morning, did you?"

"No-o."

He caught the peculiar tone in her voice and regarded her with curiosity.

She didn't want to tell him, but she did. "I heard a dog yelp last night. I was afraid he was hurt, so I came out and looked."

"But you didn't see him?"

She hesitated, fearing ridicule; then, abruptly, she told him of the luminous whiteness she'd seen across the pond.

His reaction was not one she would have expected. His face hardened, its pleasant good humor lost. "Oh," he said flatly, "that damned ghost again."

"Do you know about it?"

"You bet I do. I heard about Marthe-in-the-garden after I'd been in Mefford a couple of weeks. Our-famous-ghosts sort of thing. Every old Southern town has at least one resident ghost, sometimes two or three. There's a little old lady in a pale yellow dress who occasionally answers the door at the Wallace house, usually around Christmas. She lets the visitors in but never speaks. She takes them to the drawing room and leaves them. They'll wait awhile, then get impatient, and when they look around, get somebody's attention, it turns out that the little old lady in the yellow dress lived there more than a hundred years ago.

"But your Marthe doesn't have the charm of the lady in yellow. Marthe only walks in the garden when somebody's going to die." His voice was angry. "The first time Marthe showed up again was in June, a couple of weeks after I got settled in my tent and started digging."

He seemed to take Marthe's appearance as a personal affront, and Leah couldn't imagine why. Until he told her.

"I didn't see her myself," Kent continued. "Old Jason told me, his eyes bigger than buckets. I didn't laugh at him. I mean, he's the closest thing to living history around here, but I sure thought he was nutty, because I could tell he believed it. He had seen her. And he thought, God love him, that she'd come for him. He told me, 'Mr. Kent, I done lived a long time and my time's a-comin', I know.' I told him not to be a fool or he'd talk himself into the grave. But he just shook his head. The surprise was on both of us. I'm the one who had an accident, almost a fatal one. The first time I thought it was a coincidence. The second time, I knew it wasn't. And now you tell me you've seen the ghost, too."

They skirted a clump of oleander and came out into a clearing. Kent's head snapped up as though he'd been struck. His face twisted in anger.

The land had been cleared of trees many years ago, probably when these buildings had been built. There were six slave cabins, a barn and several outbuildings. Leah could see where Kent had been excavating, just to the back and the side of one of the slave cabins. But the twine grid wasn't neat and taut, as it had been at the first excavation. It was pulled loose and lay limp and tangled. Uneven tracks of a wheelbarrow showed where dirt fill had been rolled and dumped back into the pit.

Kent started toward the vandalized pit, then paused and glanced toward a huge cottonwood tree not far from the barn.

Leah saw a jumble of boards, haphazardly flung about.

The effect on Kent was galvanic. "What the hell!" he exploded and began to run.

CHAPTER EIGHT

In his loose-fitting Levi's and pulled-out work shirt, Kent had impressed Leah as being a little soft and out of shape, but he left her a good fifteen feet behind as he ran. He was already kneeling over a dark circular hole when she caught up to him.

"Can't see . . . surely nobody'd just wreck . . . what the hell . . ." He pulled himself back from the edge, his expression contorted from outrage and exertion. "Can't tell what's been messed up. You stay here. I'll get a flashlight from my tent."

He loped off, moving again at a surprising speed. Leah stepped a little nearer the opening and peered down. She smelled the dust and age and decay. Apparently, the well had been level with the ground, which seemed dangerous to her. Then she decided that the wall circling the top of the well had probably been removed when the decision was made to board it over. She couldn't see into the depths, so she turned her head and listened. But no sound came from below. If water lay at the bottom, it lay unmoving.

The boards had lain across the top of the well, a necessary precaution for passersby even though there couldn't be much traffic in this remote area. She wondered why Kent Ellis was so upset about the boards' removal. Of course, if he had excavated down in the well . . . Then she saw the pitons driven into one side of the hole, and the sturdy manila ropes knotted through the eyes. She looked over the edge again and discerned the rope ladder. Obviously, Kent had explored the shaft, and there was something important to him down there.

Leah shivered, though the early sun lay warmly against her shoulders. She wouldn't want to go down into a dank and musty hole—not for anything.

Kent returned with a huge flashlight and a coil of rope and knelt by the opening. When he saw the rope ladder still in place, he dropped the coil of rope to one side. "Thought they might've ripped out the ladder while they were at it." Then he swung the huge flashlight over the side and turned it on.

"Oh, hell." His voice was shaky.

Leah saw several things at once—the uneven, rockstrewn bottom of the well; chalk marks down the shaft denoting water levels; the shiny, fresh glisten of the rope ladder; and, shockingly, a limp and bloody hump of fur next to a mound of rocks.

"Bill." Kent didn't call out the little dog's name. He said it with a grim finality.

Kent sat back on his heels. "Poor little guy. Thrown out on the river to die, and now this. He was . . ." Kent paused for a moment, then continued gruffly. "He was scared spitless the first few days I had him. Then he came out of it and was friendly to everybody. Trusting." He took a deep breath. "If I just hadn't been gone so long last night! I'd driven into Charleston to pick up some stuff I needed. On the way back, I had a flat, and I didn't have a spare, so it took awhile."

"Did anyone know you were going?"

"Yeah. I left word up at the house that I'd be coming back about nine or so. I've tried to let them know whenever I'm getting back after dark so the sound of the truck won't worry them."

If someone—Cissy? John Edward? Merrick?—wanted to vandalize Kent's work, Leah thought, it wouldn't be hard to find a good time to do it. It wouldn't be hard, either, to discover that his truck had no spare.

Kent was thinking, too. "There was a nail in the right rear tire."

They looked at each other, but neither put suspicions into words.

"What time did you hear the dog?" he asked abruptly.

"It wasn't very late. I'd gone to bed early, and his cries woke me up out of that first deep sleep. I don't imagine it was much after ten."

"So if somebody wanted to mess up my stuff, he could be pretty sure the flat would keep me out of the way long enough. I didn't get back till after midnight." Kent looked toward the well. "If somebody came and started ripping stuff up, the pup could have got frisky, wanting to play. If he kicked the dog..." He turned his head and gazed down the hill, and she knew he was trying to judge how far a sound might carry in the night stillness.

If a dog hurt, if it yelped in pain, yes, that sound could carry on a still night.

Kent's face hardened. "Poor little guy," he said again. "Okay, I'm going down." He shoved the flashlight into a hip pocket, then swung agilely over the side of the well and onto the ladder.

Leah saw the top of his head descending into the murky air. Then, suddenly, he lurched violently to the left. The movement was utterly unexpected. Yet in the half instant of time that he had, Kent reacted, gaining a chance where he should have had none at all.

As the rope ladder ripped away about three feet below the lip of the well, he thrust his hands out backward and his feet out forward. With the force and strength of his body, he wedged his hands against one side of the well, his feet against the opposite wall.

Leah saw his peril. If he eased his pressure, if his hands or the soles of his boots slipped, he would crash far below on the uneven mound of rocks.

Turning, she grabbed up the coil of rope he had dropped earlier. But as he leaned over the side of the shaft, she felt a pang of horror. What good would the rope do? His hands were jammed behind him. How could he possibly catch the rope if she tossed it down? But she had to do something and do it quickly. He couldn't possibly maintain the pressure necessary to hold himself against the well walls for very long.

She almost dropped down a length of rope, hoping he could somehow manage to catch old of it. Then she stopped, her heart thudding. How could she be such a fool? If she did, Kent Ellis would be doomed because she could never support his weight.

"Hurry." He said it calmly enough, but she didn't mistake the urgency in his voice.

If she could tie the rope... She knelt and yanked at the remnants of the rope ladder, but it was securely tied through the eyes of the pitons. She couldn't pick it loose and she didn't have a knife.

Desperate, she looked around. The cottonwood tree loomed above. It was immense, and the lowest branch was out of her reach.

"Hurry." His voice was harder to hear now.

Leah damned her ineptitude. A moment later she knew what she had to do. Scrambling to her feet, she uncoiled the rope and ran to the tree. She circled it once, twice, then hurried back to the well and dropped to her knees.

"I'm going to let the rope down near your right hand. I've looped one end of it around the tree trunk to ease the strain, and I'll hold on to the other end."

She dropped the loose end of the rope as near to his right hand as she could. He watched it coming closer and closer. Then, quickly, in a superb athlete's gamble, he twisted to his right, shifting his body's pressure to his right shoulder and elbow and turning his feet at the same time. Now he was pressed sideways across the well, and his left hand was free and reaching out for the dangling rope. His fingers closed on it convulsively, but he didn't jeopardize his fragile balance. First he looped the rope around his forearm; then, cautiously, he tested his lifeline.

Leah watched, scarcely breathing, and braced her feet against the edge of the well, but the trunk of the cottonwood held the rope taut.

Sure now of his support, Kent worked his way up the rope, hand over hand, feet braced against the wall, until he was at the top and over. He collapsed on the dusty ground and drew in great heaving gulps of air. Finally, when he could talk, he sat up and looked at Leah. "Thanks, lady." His face was ashwhite. "Almost nobody ever comes this way."

If he had fallen to the bottom of the shaft, even if he'd survived the fall, he could have lain there for a long, long time.

"Why did the rope ladder break?" she asked.

In answer, he leaned over the well and fished up the short end still dangling from the pitons. He held it up, and Leah saw the neat, clean slice three-fourths of the way through the rope and the jagged tears where it had given way beneath his weight.

"What are you going to do?" she asked.

"I don't know," he said slowly. "I'll be damned if I know." He shoved a hand through his tight brown curls. "I'd go to the cops, tear this wide open, if there were something concrete to tell them."

"Cut ropes are pretty concrete."

"Yeah. And you know what the sheriff would say?"

She shook her head.

"He'd say, 'That's a shame, young man. Must be a vandal. Kids these days don't know where to stop. A lucky thing you weren't hurt.'"

"But I could tell him about hearing the dog and seeing the . . . the ghost."

Kent laughed grimly. "Sheriff Hailey's about six-four, two hundred and forty pounds. He doesn't believe in ghosts, just in colorful shades for the tourist trade. If you even hinted you thought Marthe was flesh and blood—or worse, a Devereaux up to no good—it would blow his mind. People like the Devereaux . . . well, honey, they're so far above suspicion that anyone pointing a finger at them would automatically be classified as nuts or some kind of troublemaker."

The sun was over the trees now, the air soft and steamy. Leah felt the warmth against her skin, but it didn't help against the coldness that swept through her. She might be a Devereaux, she was a Devereaux, but she was also a stranger in a strange land.

Kent got up, brushing the dirt from his jeans. He recoiled the rope, then, tied it over the cottonwood branch that had been out of Leah's reach.

She realized he intended to go back into the well. Because, of course, the dog's body was still there. She didn't watch, but she listened and knew when he'd reached the bottom. She heard him swear.

It seemed like a very long time before he started up. As he came over the edge she saw he had brought up Bill. She turned away, but he called out to her, his voice hard and angry. "Look at this—look at it!"

He laid the dog on the sandy ground. Leah saw stiffened fur and a gaping wound in the narrow throat. Thick clots of dried blood clung to the chest and forelegs.

Kent held up a bayonet. The bronze metal glistened in the sunlight except where it was stained a darkish red. "This was wedged in the rocks. It pointed up."

If Kent had fallen down the shaft, he would have been gigged like a fish, speared by the bayonet.

"It could have been passed off as an accident," Kent said. "This is period stuff, a Civil War bayonet. It was made in Charleston from melted-down bronze gates. Everybody would've said I'd found it, dug it up in the well and been so excited I probably lost my grip on the rope ladder and fell down the shaft." His eyes blazed. "You can figure it out, too, can't you? Do you suppose anybody would have noticed how very sharp the blade is? Or wondered how the dog and I both got ripped up?" He shook his head. "Hell, no. It would've been another unfortunate accident at Devereaux Plantation." He balanced the bayonet in his hand. "Somebody's too damned clever, and it isn't any ghost."

Leah stared in horror at the glistening weapon. "Did the dog fall down the well and . . ."

Kent shook his head. "No. He was lying to the side of the bayonet. Like I told you, it was wedged down in those rocks, fixed for me to land on. No, Bill must've come up on somebody when he was ripping off the boards. Maybe that was when Bill got kicked. You said you heard one yelp, then later some more. Maybe Bill nipped around at the person, and whoever it was got sore, swiped the bayonet across his throat and tossed him down." Kent frowned. "But that wasn't too smart, because it would have looked odd, both me and the dog down there dead. Maybe it was doubly clever, though. He killed the dog and tossed him down, knowing I'd find the uncovered well and be looking for Bill and go after him. Maybe the guy intended to climb down and get Bill out to bury him, then discover my body and raise the alarm."

Yes, it was clever. Clever and horrible. Evil. Someone had moved quietly in the soft-scented Carolina night, keeping to the shadows, ready to kill and destroy anyone or anything in his path.

"I guess that's what happened," Leah said slowly.

"You don't agree?" Kent's voice was sharp. "You think that bayonet just grew down there?"

"No. No, I believe someone planted it." She frowned. "But why you, Kent?"

"I don't know! But let me tell you, there's no doubt about it. Listen." He thumped an index finger against the opposite palm. "The ghost shows up the first week in June. Three days later, I'm down in the dig behind the slave cabins, and it's just God's grace I stopped working for a minute. I heard something, a different kind of sound, and I looked up." He paused and swallowed. "You see, the old chimney, a huge thing, was still standing. I'd started my pit behind it. I knew it was kind of unstable, but it was safe enough as long as nothing jolted it." His face tightened in remembrance. "I looked up, and that chimney started to fall."

He'd lunged, throwing himself to the side. An instant later, rubble five feet deep had covered the spot where he'd been working. Again, it was his agility that had saved him. If he hadn't paused for that instant, hadn't looked up . . .

Three weeks later, the ghost had walked again. Lilac had seen it that time, the white, luminous movement deep in the shadows of the willows. She'd told Old Jason.

"But when he told me, he still thought it meant his time had come. And it really didn't occur to me to link it up with my accident."

"What happened the second time?" Leah asked.

"Somebody planned for me to drown."

"But how could . . ."

"I made it easy," he said dryly. "Most evenings I'd row out into the river after I'd had supper. Then I'd put out the anchor and take a swim." He saw her expression and shrugged. "Not too bright, maybe, but I'm a good swimmer, and I didn't get too far from the boat. And it never occurred to me that anybody would cut my anchor line." He glanced toward the well. "Somebody's too damn handy with a knife around here. Anyway, that's what must have happened, and I didn't check the line before I threw it out.

"There's a hell of a current out there. That boat was already out of sight, and there I was, seventy-five yards from the bank and looking for the boat—and the current swinging away from the shore. I swam diagonally and came in a couple of miles downstream. If I weren't a strong swimmer . . ."

Once, twice, a third time. There could hardly be any question about it. Someone badly wanted to kill Kent Ellis.

"There must be a reason," Leah said.

Kent shook his head, some of the color back in his face now. He wiped his hands on his jeans. "Look, I'd better bury Bill. Wait a minute while I go get a shovel."

Why would anybody try to kill Kent Ellis? Why would anybody kill a dog? That was all Leah could think of as she waited.

Kent gave her a faint smile when he returned and began to dig a grave.

"There has to be a reason," she said again.

"Right. Nobody goes in for murder unless the stakes are pretty high." He paused for a few moments, then said, "I figure two things. One, Marthe is a smoke screen, a handy scapegoat for accidents somebody wants to happen. Two, somebody at Devereaux Plantation is a killer."

It was very quiet in the clearing.

When Leah didn't answer, Kent started digging again, the shovel thumping dully, the dry dirt rattling as it fell.

Somebody at Devereaux Plantation. That meant one out of five members of her family, Leah thought, not counting the servants.

"And perhaps," she said aloud, "that person has killed before."

She told Kent of the long-ago summer when her parents and Louisa and she had arrived on the boat. "The ghost had appeared twice that summer—and both times my grandmother was almost killed. Then the boat was lost, and the ghost wasn't seen again until this summer."

"Your grandmother went to Nice soon after your parents were lost, didn't she?"

"Yes."

"So the ghost appeared twice that summer and didn't appear again after your grandmother left."

"Do you think there's a connection?"

"Don't you?"

"I don't know what to think," Leah responded. "But Carrie hasn't had any accidents this summer—you have. And it wasn't my grandmother who died nineteen years ago, it was my parents."

Kent stopped shoveling and looked at her somberly.

"If somebody murdered your parents, why did your grandmother Shaw grab you and run away? Why didn't she call the cops?"

There it was. Out in the open. Leah licked lips that felt suddenly stiff and dry. The August sunlight poured over them in the little clearing cupped among the pine trees. Kent's shirt clung to his back. Sweat beaded her face, but inside she felt cold, cold to the bone.

Why hadn't Louisa gone to the police? What could have prompted her to gather up a small child and run away, leaving behind her own home in Atlanta, the life she'd always known, her friends and family?

"I don't know," Leah said tonelessly. Then she added, "My parents quarreled that night."

"How do you know that?"

"My cousins saw them on the dock."

"So you think . . ." His words trailed off.

"I don't know what to think." She reached down and rubbed the dusty dirt hard with her fingers. "Marthe killed Timothy, then shot herself. Didn't she?"

Kent frowned. "What does that have to do with anything?" But he saw the parallel and understood what she feared.

"Why else," she asked relentlessly, "would Louisa run away with me and let both of us be presumed dead? Why else?"

Slowly, he nodded in agreement.

Leah wanted to cry, but tears wouldn't help. She could never wash away the horror of that reality. But after all, what did it have to do with her now? Everything, her heart cried, everything. You are what you come from. If there's a weakness, a strain of darkness, within me, I must know it and face it.

Kent was absorbed in thought. "Yeah," he said abruptly, "that must have been exactly what your grandmother Shaw thought. Otherwise, her running away with you doesn't make any sense." He looked at Leah and moved quickly, dropping the shovel and taking her cold hands in his. "Hey, don't look so devastated. Just because your grandmother thought it, that doesn't mean it happened that way."

She held tightly to his hands. He was her link to sanity and faith.

"For Pete's sake," he scolded, "haven't you figured out yet that half of everything people believe is an illusion? It's easy to fool people if you set out to do it. Plus, everybody's got a different picture of reality."

Leah listened hard, wanting desperately to believe. And in the letter . . . "Kent, I hadn't told you, but Louisa was writing to Carrie when she died. She wrote that if the ghost walked again, then she had been deceived that night. She said it meant there was great evil at Devereaux Plantation."

"Evil" didn't seem too strong a word when she looked down at the little mound that marked Bill's grave and at the blood-encrusted bayonet lying beside it.

Kent squinted thoughtfully. "We have to reconstruct what happened that weekend."

"How can we do that?"

"Ask people what happened," he said simply.

They planned it out. He would tackle Lilac. The family was up to Leah. Hal didn't count, because he'd left the house early that long-ago afternoon. Farther afield, Kent would talk to the sheriff, discreetly. Leah would visit with Mrs. LeClerc, and see Old Jason when he was well enough.

Kent frowned. "I wish Jason weren't in the hospital, though we probably couldn't get anything out of him that would make any sense."

"Why not? He was certainly there. After all, he's the one who wrote to Mary Ellen and asked her to come."

"I know. But he's really old now, and he gets confused. He comes and sits by the edge of the excavations and talks about the Devereaux past and present. Sometimes he gets things mixed up—tells me things his father said, as if he himself had lived through them. One time I got him talking about Marthe and Timothy. This was after he'd spotted the ghost in June. He got real excited and said, 'Miss Marthe, she don't think it's right. She walks because they didn't bury her proper and her soul can't rest—no, it can't!'

"Jason paced up and down by the edge of the pit, and I was afraid he was going to topple right in. 'Oh, lost souls will haunt you, Mr. Kent,' he said. 'I knew it was wrong, just like my daddy knew it was wrong. He told me on his deathbed that it was wrong what happened about Miss Marthe. And I knew it wasn't true about Miss Mary Ellen, no matter what they said. And she haunts me now, lying in that cursed ground. Her soul can't rest! She's comin' for me!' I thought the old boy's mind was gone. He had them confused, Marthe and Mary Ellen."

"He actually said my mother's name?"

Kent nodded.

"I've got to talk to him," Leah said excitedly. "He must know something!"

"Maybe. Frankly, I think he's pretty well around the bend. But I don't suppose it would hurt to ask him."

Leah left Kent standing by the small grave and walked slowly back toward the house. Would it do any good to poke and pry? Or would everything she discovered lead inexorably to the same horror-laden conclusion: Marthe had killed Timothy; Mary Ellen had killed Tom.

CHAPTER NINE

When Leah reached the pond, she walked even faster. She knew now what kind of horror had waited there the night before. If she had crossed the bridge then—Her footsteps clattered across the wooden planks as images whirled in her mind: the bloody hump of fur that had been a dog, her mother's face, the storm driving in from the sea, Louisa . . .

At the foot of the rose garden, Leah looked up and saw Merrick standing on the first-floor veranda. She began to run toward him.

He met her at the bottom of the steps and caught her in his arms. "What's wrong? What's happened?"

She told him, starting with her troubled sleep the night before, the dog's yelps, and the ghost.

He nodded toward the pond. "Down there?"

"Yes."

"Don't you suppose," he said carefully, "that it's possible you imagined it? After all, you'd just awakened. Perhaps you felt frightened and—"

"I saw it," she insisted. She reached into her pocket and held out her hand. The piece of white silk glistened in the sunlight.

Merrick gave a tiny shrug. "The wind blows. That's as light as a thistle. It could have come from anywhere."

"That's not all that's happened." The words tumbled out as Leah told him of her meeting with Kent Ellis and what they had discovered at the bottom of the well.

Merrick was silent for a long moment. Then, not looking at her, he said stiffly, "Maybe Ellis's excavations made somebody mad."

"Who?"

The single word hung in the air between them.

"How should I know?" he demanded irritably. "But it has to be something like that. Otherwise, it wouldn't make any sense."

"Wouldn't it?"

Again the silence stretched between them. She waited for him to ask her what she meant.

Instead, he frowned and said, "I'll go down and talk to Ellis." Then he looked at her imploringly. "Leah, this doesn't have anything to do with us. All this talk about ghosts is stupid. You have to understand that people around here are superstitious. Somebody sees some marsh gas, and a whole new story goes around."

"I didn't see any marsh gas."

He stared down at the garden. "As for Ellis, we don't really know anything about him. Maybe he likes attention."

"Do you think he cut his dog's throat?"

"We don't know anything about him," Merrick repeated stubbornly. "Anyway, I'll go down and talk to him. Maybe he ought to stop his excavations for a while." He paused, then asked quietly, "You'll go see the plantations with me this afternoon, won't you?"

She stared at him for a long moment, at his auburn hair that shone so richly in the sunlight, at his deep blue eyes that looked at her with so much longing. He was everything she'd ever wanted in a man; she felt a link between them that could one day explode into passion. But at this moment, while she fought to believe in her parents, he refused to admit that evil existed at Devereaux Plantation.

The silence grew.

Merrick's chin jutted out. "I'll pick you up at one." Then he turned and strode off.

She stared after him, her heart twisting inside. He didn't want to believe her, and she understood why. There was such a small circle of suspects—if suspects there were. But that didn't help the ache inside her.

She looked up at the lovely old house, so proud and unvanquished. It sat out in the country in splendid isolation. There were the servants, of course. But other than the family, who would know or care that Kent Ellis was excavating at Devereaux Plantation—or where?

That left the family. Carrie Devereaux. Cissy and Hal Winfrey. John Edward.

And, of course, Merrick.

But why would he—Leah put it into words in her mind for the very first time—why would he or Cissy or John Edward have murdered Mary Ellen and Tom?

As she gazed up at the lovely mansion on the hill, she knew the answer. To inherit Devereaux Plantation, of course.

Everyone—meaning Leah's three adopted cousins—had thought Mary Ellen was well out of it when she eloped with Tom. Carrie had cut her daughter out of her will. Who would inherit? The adopted Devereaux.

Slowly, Leah climbed the broad, shallow steps and began to walk in the shadowy coolness of the west veranda. Her mind continued to spin its dreadful logic.

When Mary Ellen and Tom had arrived, perhaps one of the cousins hadn't wanted to risk an eventual healing of the breach between mother and daughter. Perhaps one of them had decided to make absolutely certain that the breach could never be healed.

Perhaps the truth was uglier yet. The ghost had already walked—and twice Carrie had been near death. Mary Ellen had announced on the windswept dock that she wouldn't leave until she knew the truth about her mother's accidents. Perhaps she had understood her cousins very well indeed and had discovered who might already have been tempted to try to gain Devereaux Plantation.

It was all so long ago and far away. How could Mary Ellen's daughter ever hope to find the truth? But if Leah didn't, dark imaginings would always exist in her mind.

Merrick, John Edward or Cissy.

One of them.

All of them?

"Leah."

She turned, startled, and saw Cissy coming out onto the porch.

"Have you had breakfast yet?" Cissy looked lovely in a thin gray cambric dress with a ruche of lace at her throat.

"No. I've been out for a walk." It was odd how true that was, yet how deceptive. Should she tell her about Kent Ellis and the dog?

Cissy came nearer, and Leah was shocked to see patches of rouge standing out on her cheeks. Dark hollows made her green eyes look huge and somehow lost.

"What's wrong?" Leah asked quickly.

Cissy looked away. "Nothing. Come, let's have breakfast."

She led the way, and after a moment, Leah followed. She had a feeling that Cissy wanted to talk to her, that she hadn't joined her just to share breakfast.

Two places were set at the breakfast table. Cissy sat where she could look down into the gardens. "John Edward's already eaten, and Aunt Carrie always eats in her room," she said absently. "Hal's still in bed."

Leah sat down. "I saw Merrick." Her voice was carefully impersonal.

Cissy shot an avid glance. "I believe Merrick's smitten with you." She said it archly.

Leah looked at her in surprise. The old-fashioned term sounded jarring. Moreover, it seemed out of character for Cissy to notice or care. So far she had treated Leah civilly but coolly, yet now she waited eagerly to hear her response to a statement clearly designed to prompt girlish confidences.

"He's very nice," Leah replied stiffly.

Cissy's fine eyebrows drew down in a little frown. "Don't you like him?"

"I like him very much. I like everyone."

As she said this, she knew it wasn't true. She didn't have any great liking for John Edward or Cissy or Hal, and what she felt for Merrick was a magnificent caring. She wanted to be near him, to love him. The intensity of her feelings shocked and overwhelmed her. She'd never seen him until just a few days ago. How could she respond this way so quickly?

Because it was right. She felt its rightness deep within. Whether their relationship ever came to fruition, she knew there was a bond between them that nothing could destroy. It had happened as suddenly, and as violently, as a spring storm.

Yet now she sat talking to Cissy, mouthing words she didn't mean while a welter of emotions churned within her.

"It's really very nice to have you here," Cissy said.

Leah felt certain that Cissy didn't mean a word of it, though her face was stretched in a smile. The smile did little to improve her mottled complexion. Leah realized with a sense of shock that Cissy looked wretched. Her lovely hair was swept up in a coronet of braids. Her makeup was flawless, her dress exquisitely tailored, but her eyes were big green pools of misery in her strained face.

"Something's wrong, Cissy," Leah said gently. "Tell me what it is."

Cissy motioned with her hand, and Leah realized that Henry was rolling up a serving cart. He poured coffee and served them Belgian waffles and fresh strawberries.

When he had gone, Cissy said, so quietly that Leah could scarcely hear, "I'm frightened."

Whatever she had expected, it wasn't this. She would have judged Cissy to be hard as hickory, impervious to stress, coolly competent in all situations.

But now Cissy stared at her with wide eyes, and Leah knew that something dreadful lurked in the corridors of her mind. Abruptly, without warning, she thought of the horrid, dank air wafting slowly up from the uncovered well where Bill had died and where Kent Ellis had nearly been killed. Could Cissy know something about that? Or were her fears tied to the nineteen-year-old disappearance?

"Tell me." Leah's voice was sharp.

Cissy leaned across the table. "I talked to Tetine this morning. Do you know her? She's my little maid."

Leah remembered glimpsing her in an upper hallway. "Yes, I know who you mean."

Cissy swallowed, then said huskily, "Last night Tetine saw Marthe." Her face reflected strain and something more. Was it really fear? She stared at Leah, her eyes almost bulging. "Tetine was coming home late. She parked in the garage and began to walk."

The garage. That was where Henry had put Leah's rented Vega. The garage sat to the east of the gardens; the servant quarters were to the west, not far from the tower. So Tetine would have been walking through the shadowy gardens.

"I wonder why I didn't see Tetine."

Cissy looked at her intently. "Were you in the gardens last night?"

"Yes. But I didn't see Tetine."

"Did you see Marthe?" Cissy demanded.

Leah hesitated, then said determinedly, "I don't believe in ghosts."

Cissy's eyes were even more wide and strained. "You did see her!"

"I saw something," Leah admitted. "But let me show you what I found this morning." She proffered the little scrap of white silk.

Cissy didn't touch it. Like Merrick, she said, "That doesn't mean anything. The wind could have blown it there." She stared down at her hands which she was twisting restlessly in her lap. "Someone always dies when Marthe walks in the garden. Someone always—"

"Hush," Leah interrupted almost angrily.

Cissy gave her a wild, driven look. "You don't believe it, do you? I tell you, we must all beware. Death is coming." Abruptly, she pushed back her chair and rose, half stumbling, and fled down the veranda.

Leah stared after her. Despite her certainty that some human agency had moved that ghostly white luminescence, she felt a rush of fear. Obviously, Cissy believed both in the ghost and that death was coming to Devereaux Plantation.

Her fist closed around the little piece of silk. That was her proof, whether Merrick and Cissy could accept it or not. Marthe didn't walk in the garden. A living, breathing someone, with a twisted spirit and an evil goal, was behind that glowing white appearance.

In only one respect did Leah agree with Cissy. She understood only too well that the ghostly charade forecast death. Three times death had waited for Kent Ellis. Somehow she and Kent must figure out what was happening at Devereaux Plantation and why.

She ate her breakfast without tasting a bite. It was a task to be done while she thought—and worried. Why did Merrick refuse to listen to her? That answer came too easily. He'd been there the night her mother and father had disappeared. He'd only been a boy, but he'd been there, and he must have known how his brother and sister had felt—and still felt—about their cousin. Every time Leah told Merrick some new fact that she'd learned, he downplayed it, tried to put a good face on it. And he always turned attention away from Devereaux Plantation. Even now he was talking to Kent and, she knew, seeking some reason to believe that Kent—and not anyone named Devereaux—was part of the ugliness.

Wearily, she totted up what she knew. The ghost had reappeared after an absence of many years, and Louisa had begun that letter to Carrie. What link could there be between the ghost and her parents? And why would the ghost appear now and threaten Kent? There could not possibly be a link between her parents and the archaeologist.

She shook her head wearily. None of that made sense. And she didn't want to think of other things, either. Niggling at the back of her mind was the fear that she didn't want to verbalize—that Old Jason had equated Marthe and Mary Ellen when everyone knew that Marthe had killed her lover.

Leah closed her mind to that; she wouldn't think it again. Not ever.

Still, she couldn't help wondering what the truth was about her mother. Had she been loving, kind and brave? Or angry and vengeful, a hellcat?

Leah threw her napkin down and pushed her chair away from the breakfast table. She couldn't ask anyone here at the house, but she could ask Mrs. LeClerc. Perhaps that would help her resolve the question in her own mind.

She had to know about her mother. She had to know, because she and Mary Ellen and Marthe were linked, and that was what Mrs. LeClerc had meant when she told Leah that she had a fated face.

"Miss Leah."

Absorbed in her thoughts, she hadn't heard Henry approach. Startled, she looked up. "Yes, Henry?"

"If you've finished your breakfast, Miss Carrie would like to see you."

She found her grandmother propped up in a huge bed that made her look even smaller and frailer. Leah bent down to kiss her cheek, and the old lady smiled.

"Did you see the gardens this morning? Henry said you'd gone for a walk."

Leah smiled and nodded.

"Aren't they lovely in the early-morning light?"

Leah hesitated, then plunged into her story, not only of the ghostly apparition the night before but of Kent Ellis and his dog and his accidents.

Carrie Devereaux seemed to shrink against her pillows, but her great black eyes stared indomitably at Leah. "There is no ghost."

"I know, Grandmother. I don't believe there is a ghost, either," she agreed quietly. "But there is someone at Devereaux Plantation who wants all of us to believe in a ghost."

Carrie protested. "No," she said sharply. "It's all a coincidence. As for that young man, he wants to hear old stories, so when a superstitious maid says she's seen Marthe, he believes it. As for his accidents, they sound like accidents to me." She swept over Leah's murmur of dissent. "That chimney'd been leaning a little more every year. And he probably didn't tie his anchor securely." Then she stared out her window at the double line of live oaks curving down to the river, her mouth set tightly.

"Someone cut the rope ladder in the well," Leah said firmly. "I saw it."

Her grandmother turned back to her and reached out to take her hand. "Dear God, Leah, what's happening to us?"

"I don't know. But we have to face it. We have to try and find out."

Carrie's hand tightened on Leah's. "Be careful. Promise me.

"I'll be careful, I promise."

And she intended to keep that promise. She intended to be very careful indeed. She had warned Kent to be cautious, and now she had warned her grandmother. The three of them would pursue their search for the truth, but they would all be wary.

Forewarned is forearmed.

CHAPTER TEN

Leah ran lightly down the stairs. She had so much to do. First she would talk to Mrs. LeClerc—

John Edward stood at the foot of the stairs, looking up.

As she reached him, he said, "You're in a very great hurry this morning." His eyes looked at her searchingly.

Tired of pretense, she lifted her chin. "I'm going to talk to Mrs. LeClerc. About my mother."

"I don't think that's very wise."

She knew then that her face didn't evoke memories of a long-lost love. His eyes were cold, and the enmity he felt was clear. He did indeed hate the woman who had left him.

"I'm going to find out."

"You may regret it."

"Then why don't you tell me what she was really like?"

The question throbbed between them.

"Leave it alone." His voice was hard and cold. "You keep on and on, and what's the good of it? Mary Ellen and Tom are dead. Let them rest in peace."

That was easy for him to say. R.I.P., that was what they carved on gravestones years ago. But Mary Ellen and Tom had no gravestone, only the ghostly gray sailing sloop in stone, a memorial—and a lie. How could they rest in peace?

"She came back here because of the ghost and Grandmother's accidents," Leah said harshly. "She came back because she thought someone was trying to kill Grandmother."

John Edward was shaking his head.

Her eyes narrowed. "All right. Then you tell me why she came."

She waited, holding her breath. Would he answer? Would he finally reveal something more of that long-ago visit?

"It isn't that simple," he said slowly.

She waited for more.

"You see, Mary Ellen was clever. And she loved Devereaux Plantation."

"What are you saying, John Edward?"

"She was behind the ghost."

Leah's breath came out in a sharp, irritated spurt. "That's crazy. There's no way she could've been the ghost. Why, everybody agrees she hadn't been back to Mefford for a long time."

"She didn't have to come back."

Leah raised an eyebrow. "So not only is she a ghost, but she manages it by long distance? Some kind of telekinesis, no doubt."

John Edward's jaw hardened, but he spoke levelly enough. "No. It's a lot simpler than that. I'd bet every penny I have that she managed it through Cornelia, her old maid."

"Who's Cornelia?"

"She took care of Mary Ellen from the time she was a little girl."

Leah frowned. "Is she here now? I haven't heard of her."

John Edward shook his head. "She died two years ago. But Cornelia would've done anything for Mary Ellen. Anything. I can see how Mary Ellen figured it. She talked Cornelia into waving something white down in the garden, and that got the talk started about the ghost. Aunt Carrie's accidents—and that's all they were, accidents—just added fuel to the fire. Mary Ellen knew Old Jason was spooky and that he'd write or call her if he got scared enough. He did. So that gave her an excuse to insist to Tom that they come."

"But why?" Leah demanded. "Why this silly charade?"

"Oh, it wasn't silly," he retorted. "She never did anything silly. Don't you understand? She wanted to have Tom, but she also wanted to have Devereaux Plantation—and she was going to do her damnedest to worm her way back into her mother's good graces." He paused, then shook his head. "But it didn't work."

No, it didn't. Instead, she and Tom had quarreled and . . .

"There was no reason for my mother to . . . to shoot my father," Leah said carefully.

"Reason?" John Edward shrugged. "Mary Ellen was dramatic. Perhaps she took the dueling pistols and never intended to shoot anyone. Perhaps she aimed one of them at herself. She would do things like that, you know, and Tom might have reached out and grabbed for it. Perhaps they struggled. And if the pistol went off and killed him, she would've been maddened by grief. She was like that, you know."

Leah didn't know. All she knew about her mother was what she'd been told.

"Anyway," John Edward said reasonably, "it doesn't matter after all these years. Stop worrying about it, Leah. You've found your family, and everything's going well for you. Enjoy it. Don't let the past ruin everything."

Everything he said made sense. She thought of his words as she walked slowly out of the house and down into the gardens. So why didn't she follow his advice? Because she didn't like him and didn't believe he had her best interests at heart, no matter how fine and kind his advice might sound. Maybe she was stiff-necked. They said that about Mary Ellen, too. But Leah wanted to know the truth even if everyone else insisted her quest was impossible. She wanted to be able to look at Mary Ellen's young face in the pictures that remained of her today—and look at her own face in the mirror—and feel that she'd done her best to solve the mystery of her mother and father's fate.

The oyster shells crackled underfoot. The sweet, heavy scent of the roses swirled around her in the light breeze. It was already hot and humid in the garden. Leah looked down at the sloping land and suddenly wished she had a sketchbook in hand. Could she capture the lushness of the greenery and the bright, heavy blooms? Her eyes traveled slowly across the garden, then paused at the shabby gray tower. She frowned.

The tower didn't belong in the painting she saw in her mind. It added a disturbing note, a feeling of oppression and decay. Cissy was right, Leah thought suddenly. They should pull the tower down, no matter how old it was. The tower was dark and menacing. It didn't belong.

She walked slowly toward it. It loomed above her and drew her slowly up the path. She didn't really want to go near it. She should turn toward the garage.

This was where Marthe had waited for Timothy more than one hundred years ago. What had happened when they met? A quarrel? And then the sharp report of a pistol. How much later had the pistol sounded again? Blood must have stained the flooring, perhaps seeped through cracks to drip slowly into the earth.

Leah stopped and stared at the chained door. She would talk to Grandmother about the tower and see if they couldn't take it down. But would it help to do that? Stories would circulate as long as anyone knew about Marthe and Timothy. There would be those who said it was a sad tale, but the Devereaux had always been doomed—at least some of them.

Old stories and new stories.

Then Leah heard a sound and lifted her head to listen.

Snip, snip, snip.

She left the path and began to circle the tower.

Snip, snip, snip.

Leah stopped short, and her breath ached in her chest. She saw it all in one glance and understood. She didn't know why it was so shocking, because she'd known the grave was there. Her grandmother had told her that Marthe was buried by the tower in unhallowed ground.

Still, it shocked her to the core when she came around the side of the tower and saw Cissy kneeling beside the small earthen mound and carefully, slowly, clipping the grass that covered Marthe's grave.

Cissy leaned forward, one gloved hand resting on the ground, the other holding the clippers. She was intent upon her task, her face grave. But her brilliant red hair glistened like fire in the sunlight. She had changed into a pale lilac pantsuit and looked very much the lady of the manor, engaged in light gardening.

But she gardened a grave.

Cissy's head swung around. She shaded her face with her hand and regarded Leah with cool green eyes. "I didn't hear you coming."

"Sorry. I hope I didn't startle you."

"No." Cissy continued to look at her, waiting.

"I don't like the tower," Leah said baldly.

Cissy's mouth moved a little and she glanced up at the tower. "It's dangerous. I told you that. It should be torn down, but Carrie won't hear of it."

"Perhaps I should talk to her about it, too."

Cissy's face stiffened, and Leah realized she had made a mistake. Cissy would find it offensive to believe that Leah, the newcomer, could persuade Carrie Devereaux where she, Cissy, had failed.

"Carrie's very stubborn," Cissy said shortly. A bright red flush stained her cheeks, indicating her anger.

More to distract Cissy than anything else, Leah asked, "Is this Marthe's grave?"

"Yes," she said briskly. She reached out and yanked a weed from the shell border. "The gardeners won't touch it, so I have to do it."

"Why won't they touch it?"

Cissy snipped down a clump of grass near the headstone. "Oh, they're so superstitious," she said carelessly. "I suppose they think Marthe will jump out and say boo." Her tone was contemptuous.

Remembering Cissy's stark fear at breakfast earlier, Leah was surprised. "So you really don't believe Marthe walks?"

Cissy's shoulders drew in. When she looked up at Leah, her face was suddenly pinched and had paled. "The ghost . . ." She looked down at the grave. "I never think of Marthe as being here. I always picture her walking in the garden, by the willows." She began to clip again, quickly. Then she paused and looked up at Leah again, her expression grim. "It isn't superstitious to be frightened when the ghost walks in the gardens."

"She walked there because she missed Timothy," Leah said quietly.

"Before she died?" Cissy asked.

"Yes. Of course." Leah shook her head. "I can't believe she'd do it."

"Do what?"

"Kill the man she loved," Leah said huskily.

"Oh, I can. From what they say of her."

"What do they say?"

"She was like so many of the Devereaux." Cissy rocked back on her heels and shaded her face with her hand. "You have to remember that it's an old, old family. Perhaps too many cousins intermarried. I don't know. But there's a strain of wildness in the Devereaux." She frowned thoughtfully. "Maybe it's arrogance, pride gone bad. But they will have their way no matter what the cost. They say Marthe was lovely. She had a high-bridged nose, a delicate face, flowing black hair and deep violet eyes." Cissy studied Leah. "Like you," she said. "Like you and Mary Ellen. So she was beautiful. Usually, she'd smile and her words were sweet, but sometimes that dark strain would show. She'd pace on the veranda in the wind and the rain, her hair streaming behind her. They do say once she threatened to jump from the tower when she'd quarreled with Randolph."

"How awful."

Cissy shrugged and turned back to the grave and began to clip again. "It was a long time ago."

Leah stared at the moss-covered stone. She could scarcely make out Marthe's name. Yes, it was a long time ago, and it shouldn't matter at all today. But it did. Marthe and her mother were dead and gone, but their lives and deaths still touched Leah.

She knew that when Cissy spoke of the wildness in the Devereaux, she wasn't talking of Marthe alone. She was talking about Mary Ellen, too.

"John Edward thinks my mother was behind the appearances of the ghost that summer," Leah said abruptly. "He thinks she did it so Jason would ask her to come home."

Cissy sat immobile, her face as still as the gravestone. Only the clippers moved. "Is that what John Edward told you?" she asked finally.

"Yes."

There was a long silence. Then she shook her head. "I don't think so. The ghost came and Aunt Carrie almost died. I know Mary Ellen was wild and crazy, but she wouldn't have tried—"

Leah interrupted hotly, "Of course she wouldn't. Of course not. John Edward didn't mean that at all. He meant that Mary Ellen wanted to come home. That's all." She stared down at Cissy, and anger flooded her. "What do you mean, Mary Ellen was wild and crazy? She was young and happy and in love, and she cared about her mother. That's what she was like!"

Leah turned and began to run, but not before she had one last glimpse of Cissy's face. The woman's mouth was twisted in disdain, and her cool green eyes were full of a dark and ugly knowledge.

Leah ran as fast as she could.

No matter how fast she ran, she couldn't escape the frightful visions that swirled in her mind.

CHAPTER ELEVEN

As Leah drove the Vega into town on her way to see Mrs. LeClerc, she thought about her unpleasant encounters with Cissy and John Edward. Did Merrick know what his brother and sister thought? She felt a sense of estrangement. If he knew and hadn't told her, what did that mean? And underlying the worry that throbbed in her mind was a clear and present sense of danger—danger for Kent Ellis, for her, and for her grandmother. But they already knew there was danger; they weren't fools. They would be careful, and she would take special pains to protect her grandmother.

She parked by the garden wall of Mrs. LeClerc's house, then hesitated. Did she really want to know what this old lady could tell her? Then she recalled what her grandmother had said. The Devereaux had courage.

She walked through the garden and mounted the broad front steps.

Mrs. LeClerc herself answered the door. She looked for a long moment at Leah, then gestured for her to come inside and led the way to the drawing room.

"You're pale, child."

Leah looked away from Mrs. LeClerc's shrewd brown eyes and glanced around the comfortable room. The walls were paneled in native cypress, the mellow tan wood rubbed to a high gloss.

Mrs. LeClerc followed her gaze. "It used to be painted blue," she sniffed. "Natural wood wasn't fine enough then. Now, everything the older, the better. My nephew spent two months sanding down the walls. The historical society takes tourists through just to see my walls." Her eyes fastened on Leah again. "If you scrape down far enough, sometimes you find good wood. Then again, sometimes it's rotten."

"Bad blood and good blood," Leah said abruptly. "What did you mean?"

The old lady sat down in a huge wing chair and hunched herself up like a battered bird, one shoulder higher than the other. But her brown eyes, so bright, didn't waver.

"If you scrape away paint," Mrs. LeClerc answered obliquely, "you expose the grain and, sometimes, a flaw or a weakness. Paint can be used to cover things up, you know." Her bony head nodded rapidly. "Oh, yes, paint covers things up, and time and words do, too."

Leah almost held her breath. She felt that Mrs. LeClerc was coming closer to what she wanted to say, yet Leah had a sense of caution. If she moved too quickly, spoke too sharply, the old lady would flutter away, out of touch, out of reach.

"You said mine was a fated face. Why did you say that, Mrs. LeClerc?"

The elderly woman struggled up out of her chair, using her cane as a fulcrum, and stumped rapidly across the room.

Leah was afraid she had lost her, that she was leaving, but Mrs. LeClerc went directly to an old Sheraton secretary and pulled down the lid. She opened a drawer on the left and lifted out a japanned box of brilliant ebony with a rose petal inlay. She also picked up a tiny key from the drawer.

"I found this box at the bottom of a horsehide trunk in the attic. The trunk belonged to Avery LeClerc. He was a lieutenant in Lee's army and was killed at Gettysburg two months after Marthe died." She inserted the key into the box, turned it and lifted the lid. Then she held the opened box out to Leah.

Leah gently lifted out a crumpled woman's gray leather glove, still soft to the touch. It was finely sewn with an open-work design on the back and had tiny mother-of-pearl buttons at the wrist. She looked questioningly at Mrs. LeClerc, who nodded back at the box.

Beneath the glove was a folder, its edges yellow with age. Carefully, Leah lifted it out and opened it.

Mrs. LeClerc said eagerly, "They used to come in wagons so they could carry all their paraphernalia—the powder, the wet plates and all the chemicals they needed. They would come around to the different plantations. It was all the rage then because it was so new, and everybody wanted to have their pictures made. . . ."

She chattered on about how most of the early photographs had been lost during the war; and, of course, everyone knew that Randolph Devereaux had everything of Marthe's destroyed by fire. This was the only photograph of Marthe. When Mrs. LeClerc found it, she felt that it had belonged to Avery and must have been important to him, and she decided to keep it in the LeClerc family. After all, Marthe's family had turned against her. She didn't know how or when Avery had obtained the picture, but he must have had it with him at Gettysburg. She thought there must have been a story there. And wasn't Marthe a beautiful girl?

Leah couldn't answer. She was staring at another very familiar face. A cold edge of fear rippled through her.

Marthe sat stiffly, formally, as was the custom, her hands folded primly in her lap, her head high, her slender throat emphasized by the decollete gown that fell away from her shoulders. She held a bouquet of daisies and forget-me-nots, tied with a thin velvet bow.

In the portrait in the Devereaux dining room, Mary Ellen's dress was the soft white of a debutante's gown. The bodice of Marthe's dark dress was paneled with lace, the waist cinched with a sash; the background of the photograph was a swag of velvet between two imitation marble columns. But Marthe's face was interchangeable with that of Mary Ellen—and with Leah's. She had known from what everyone said that she and Marthe looked alike, but the old photograph made it all so clear.

"A fated face." Leah said it faintly.

Marthe Devereaux, dead by her own hand. Mary Ellen Devereaux Shaw . . .

Leah turned to Mrs. LeClerc. "You said there was love and hate and no one knew the truth of it. What did you mean? What do you think happened to my mother and father?"

"I knew Mary Ellen from the time she was a tiny girl," Mrs. LeClerc said slowly. "There was always a wildness about her. She would ride alone for hours. She would sail a tiny boat down the river and into the sound and laugh when Carrie worried. She was never afraid of anything. Never." Mrs. LeClerc reached out and touched Leah with a claw-like hand. "It's too dangerous, my dear, to be without fear."

Without fear. Was that the key to her mother's fate? Or was the truth darker than that?

"John Edward said my mother was a hellcat when she was crossed," Leah said.

"I wouldn't have wished to face her when she was angry," Mrs. LeClerc said. She took the picture of Marthe and gently replaced it in the japanned box. "There were whispers after The New Star was lost. Some said there had been a quarrel. An old friend of mine said her maid told her that lights had been seen that night, flashing through the rain from the tower, and there was the clank of shovels and a wailing sound. The maid could only have heard about that from some of the servants at Devereaux Plantation." Mrs. LeClerc sighed, her shoulders slumped. "They're all gone now, those old friends. I'll be gone soon."

Leah left her resting in the wing chair, lost in a reverie. After the dimness of the cypress-paneled drawing room, she blinked when she stepped out into the high sunshine of midday and the pulsating heat. Deep within, she carried with her the chill of the old house and that somber interview.

Was it the uncanny resemblance that haunted her? Or the uneasiness of recalling long-past emotions? She felt a deep sense of dread. Would she regret it if she discovered the truth of what had really happened?

Leah parked the Vega in the same spot outside the historical society where she'd left it the first time. But she wasn't the same person who had parked there then. She was going to the newspaper office. Already she was beginning to recognize landmarks. She paused outside the door to the Courier and saw her face reflected in the plate glass. Her face, Marthe's, Mary Ellen's. The three of them were so inextricably linked. She yanked the door toward her, and the reflection wavered and was gone.

A polite girl from behind the counter led her upstairs to the second floor and a back room that held the old files. There were mounds of material on the Devereaux.

She read very carefully the stories on the disappearance of The New Star and the obituaries of her parents, Louisa and herself. A search for the boat hadn't begun until almost a week after the hurricane, when Louisa's sister in Atlanta had raised an inquiry. When no trace had been found of the boat or its passengers, The New Star was presumed lost and all aboard drowned.

It wouldn't have been hard for Louisa to disappear. Perhaps she'd sailed the boat to New Orleans and found a buyer who had not heard of the search or who had welcomed a bargain and hadn't inquired too closely into the circumstances. The sale would have brought a modest sum of money, enough for Louisa to slip quietly into a small Texas town and begin a new life as an antiques dealer. How pressing, how utterly compelling must have been her reason!

At every turn, Leah faced a warning to stop probing, to leave the past alone for fear she might find an ugliness she wouldn't want to face. She replaced the clippings, then walked slowly down the stairs and out into the heat.

All the way back to Devereaux Plantation, she struggled with nightmarish conjectures. Had her mother and father quarreled bitterly? Those pistols missing from the library—had Mary Ellen taken them?

Leah turned the car up the narrow, dusty road, plunging into the vivid green depths. The sudden chill in the dank tunnel of vegetation matched the chill in her heart. When she braked beside the immense garage, which was the former carriage house, she wondered if she should make some excuse to leave Devereaux Plantation, to escape from her doubts and fears.

Then she saw Merrick striding down the path toward her, carrying a basket in one hand. He wore a pale blue polo shirt, khakis and loafers.

He waved and smiled, and her heart pounded. The way he smiled made her forget her doubts and fears.

"Did you forget?" he called out. "We're going to Ashwood today! I packed a picnic lunch."

"Did you really?"

"Actually, Henry did it with the cook's help. It will be good. Come on, Leah, let's go." He stowed the basket into the back of his station wagon.

As they drove, she studied his firm profile. He had such a strong face. She felt safe with him, secure. But could she tell him what she had learned this morning? She didn't want to now. She wanted to push the ugliness away and enjoy the afternoon.

"It's over the next rise," he said, and his eagerness was infectious.

She, too, looked ahead expectantly.

He gave her a sudden, swift look full of hopefulness, and she knew instinctively that this wasn't just another stop on the tourist trail. For some reason, it was terribly important to Merrick that she be pleased.

She leaned forward and caught the first glimpse of the house as the station wagon topped the hill. He slowed the car and brought it to a stop.

The white frame house stood on a high foundation and faced southwest. Like Devereaux Plantation, it, too, looked down a sloping hill to the river. Deep verandas extended along the front of the house on both the first and second stories. Sturdy Ionic columns supported the verandas.

"It's beautiful," Leah said softly. "Even lovelier than Devereaux House."

Merrick reached out and took her hand. "Do you really think so?" he asked, a note of anxiety in his voice.

"Oh, Merrick, I love it. It's a perfect house."

"Wait until you see the inside."

He started the car and drove downhill, then up again, pulling to a stop in a graveled turnaround in front of the double front steps. "We'll come back and get our lunch later. I want to show you Ashwood first."

They got out of the station wagon and went up the steps. Merrick unlocked the immense, hand-carved front door. An ornamental fanlight above the door spewed golden sunlight into the wide entry hall. A muted Persian rug, all browns and golds and tans, covered much of the hand-cut wooden floor. A delicate, free-standing stairway curved upward out of sight.

He took her into every room including a music room with an eighteenth-century spinet and his office with an antique roll top desk.

Finally, breathless, she climbed with him up narrow back steps to a cupola that looked down on a sweep of garden as lovely in its own way as any at Devereaux Plantation. Ferns, oleanders, wisteria and honeysuckle grew in ordered profusion.

Leah leaned forward, holding tight to the low railing. "Merrick, it's all so incredibly lovely!"

"You really do like it," he said in delight.

"Yes."

"I knew you would."

"So this is your home."

He nodded. "It was a ramshackle ruin fifteen years ago. I started work on it than, and I've restored every bit of it myself."

He told her of his efforts as they walked downstairs. She listened, but mostly she was terribly aware of his nearness.

They carried the picnic basket to the garden and settled in a wood-roofed gazebo that offered a view of the river.

"A glass of wine, Leah?"

She accepted the slender glass of chilled Chardonnay with a smile and felt a surge of excitement when his hand touched hers.

As they ate the fresh chicken sandwiches and finished them off with a light peach pastry, Leah tried so hard to control her feelings that she fell silent and had nothing to say.

When they were packing up the hamper and he stood so near, she realized that he, too, had nothing to say.

Abruptly, he reached for her and drew her into his arms. His mouth pressed against her cheek, and he spoke softly. The breath of his words touched her like flame.

"Leah, Leah, I've wanted to hold you ever since I first saw you. You'll think I'm crazy. You've known me for such a short time, but I knew I wanted you when I first saw you."

Her arms slipped up his back, and she lifted her face to look into his eyes. "Merrick . . ." Then there was no more time for thought or words. His mouth covered hers in a deep, satisfying kiss. Nothing existed in the world but the two of them and the growing desire that flamed between them.

Finally, feeling that she teetered on the edge of an emotional abyss, Leah drew gently back. She wanted to stay in his arms, but she knew she must have more time. She couldn't let herself be swept completely out of control. Not yet. No matter how much her body ached for his.

Merrick smiled happily, and she watched the dimple move at the corner of his mouth. She wanted to touch that corner with her tongue, then trace his lips and explore his mouth.

She steeled her face and her will.

"Leah, you do care. You do," he murmured.

"Merrick, let's take our time. Let's get to know each other."

His smile deepened. "I want to know you. All of you."

A tiny flush strained her cheeks, and she lowered her eyes.

Then his smile faded, and he looked serious and uncertain. "Leah . . ." He released her from his embrace. "Leah, let's walk in the garden. There is something I have to tell you."

They walked arm in arm, and she delighted in the feeling of companionship, the touching warmth.

He cleared his throat and took a deep breath. "Leah, I was married once."

She drew away from him just a little. Some of the glory seeped out of the afternoon.

Suddenly he looked tired and vulnerable. "Does it matter too much?" he asked.

"I don't know," she said slowly. "Tell me about her."

They began to walk again. "We met in college. After we married, it turned out she wanted to live in Atlanta and be a model. She hated Ashwood."

Leah half turned to look at the house up on the hill. "Did you love Ashwood more than you loved her?"

Merrick winced at that. "I'd told her about Ashwood before we got married. And then when we came here, she said it was a hideous old wreck and we should get a new house in town." He kicked at a loose stone, and it popped into a small pool nearby and sank. "Ashwood is part of me. Don't you see that?" He shook his head wearily. "We were too young, I guess. We both knew it was a mistake. It only lasted a year."

He reached for her hands and held them tight. His vivid blue eyes implored her. "Leah, until I saw you, I'd never had any desire to marry again."

She wanted to interrupt, to say this was too much too soon, but he rushed on.

"We're meant for each other, you and I. I've known it from the first moment I saw you. You and I together, here at Ashwood."

Leah knew it was madness, but she didn't care. To be in the circle of his arms was enough for the moment. And she wanted it to be so; she wanted it to be true that she and Merrick were meant for each other.

Was this how her mother and father had felt when they met? If so, how had that love ended?

Merrick pulled her close, held her tight for a long moment, then eased his embrace to smile down at her. "Tell me what you are thinking."

Leah looked up into his face and the eyes that fascinated her. Then she sighed. "I'm thinking of my parents." She swallowed and glanced away. "And of Marthe and Timothy."

Gently, his hand tilted her chin around until their eyes met again. "Why?"

She veered away from that question. "Mrs. LeClerc said I had a fated face. She said that blood tells. Oh, Merrick, do you think it does?"

He caressed her cheek with his knuckles, and the touch inflamed her. "You have a lovely face. That's all I know and all I need to know."

She drew her breath in sharply. "You believe it, don't you?"

Now it was he who didn't meet her gaze. "Leah, leave it alone."

"You think my mother killed my father?" Anguish throbbed in her voice.

His hands gripped her shoulders. Hard. "It was nineteen years ago. No one can ever know what really happened."

"But that's what you believe," she said emptily.

Slowly, the pressure of his hands eased. "I don't know what I believe. But to think anything else . . ."

They still stood close together, but the closeness they had shared so recently was gone.

Each of them, Leah realized, had private fears and secret horrors. She grappled with the monstrous idea that her mother had slain her father, for why else had Louisa fled, taking her to Texas? But Merrick had his fears, too. If Louisa had been mistaken that night, then what had become of Mary Ellen and Tom?

Merrick reached out and pulled her back into his arms, almost roughly. "Leah, it doesn't matter what happened then. What matters to us is now." His lips touched hers hungrily. After only a moment's pause, she began to kiss him in return, welcoming the heat of their passion against the coldness in her mind.

Finally, as before, it was she who broke them apart. "Let's walk, Merrick," she said shakily.

They didn't refer to her parents again. Instead, they strolled through the gardens and later drove down winding roads and took a rowboat out on the river. They talked about themselves and made important discoveries. She hated beer. He liked skydiving. She read American writers. He didn't like ballet. They both loved the symphony. And their eyes said so much more than their words.

Merrick called the house and excused her from dinner. Then they drove to Hilton Head Island and ate at the Old Fort Pub. He introduced her to okra gumbo and Gullah shrimp Creole. The Old Fort Pub overlooked Skull Creek, near the remains of a federal fort. It was only after a leisurely dinner, when they walked across a footbridge to look at a mound that represented the last of the federal works, that Leah once again felt the pull of the past. Still, she did her best to keep her fears at bay. She was young and falling in love.

They drove the long way back to Devereaux Plantation, Leah

sitting close to Merrick and wishing they could stay like this forever. By the time they reached the avenue lined with live oaks, the moon was high in the sky above the house, and it was hard to believe that evil existed in such a beautiful place.

As Merrick pulled the station wagon up by the steps, Leah considered telling him what Cissy and John Edward and Mrs. LeClerc had told her that morning. But when he came around and opened her door to help her out, she went straight into his arms, and she knew she didn't want to mar this perfect evening.

He cupped her face in his hands and kissed her, so lightly this time that it was almost more stirring than the kisses they'd shared earlier. Leah had to force herself inside at once.

"Good night," she said breathlessly.

"Good night," he murmured.

As she watched his taillights recede, she knew she would soon make a fateful decision.

She walked slowly up the shadowed steps, a smile on her face. Had anyone ever fallen in love so swiftly and so completely? She thought of the life they would share at Ashwood, loving all that was beautiful from the past while building their own shining future.

After she had entered the house, walking quietly so as not to disturb any one who might be in bed, she saw a bar of light from the partially open library door and heard the rumble of John Edward's voice.

She certainly didn't want to talk to him or any of the others now. This was her night to glory in the beginning of love. It would diminish the perfection of her evening to speak to anyone else.

She was just opposite the library door, her goal to slip quietly up the staircase, when she heard John Edward clearly.

"Are they still gone?" he asked.

"Still gone," his sister replied.

The tone of their voices shocked Leah. He sounded sardonic, and Cissy's voice was thick with satisfaction.

He laughed. "I never thought we'd be in Merrick's debt. But he's really swept her off her feet, hasn't he?"

Leah knew they were talking about her. The happiness she carried with her shriveled like a day-old flower.

"He's done a beautiful job," Cissy agreed.

Blindly, Leah ran up the stairs to her room. With the door shut behind her, she leaned back against it and stared emptily across the room. She didn't cry. It hurt too much to cry.

Yes, she thought bitterly, Merrick had done a beautiful job indeed.

CHAPTER TWELVE

The next morning, Leah applied her makeup carefully shading the blush just so, trying to hide the telltale dark smudges beneath her eyes. She paused and stared into the mirror. It was such an old mirror that her reflection wavered, giving her an insubstantial air.

It wasn't hard to imagine her mother looking into this mirror. And Marthe.

A knock sounded on her door.

When she opened it she saw Henry standing there. "You have a telephone call. Miss Leah. There's a phone in the upper hall."

"Thank you, Henry."

She walked slowly down the hall to an alcove in which a telephone sat on a table. She hesitated for a long moment, then lifted the receiver. "Hello?"

"Leah, I've planned a wonderful day." Merrick's voice sounded confident and happy.

Her heart twisted. "I'm sorry," she said stiffly, "but there are some things I need to do today."

The pause on the other end of the line was absolute.

"Leah, what's wrong?"

She heard footsteps and looked up to see Cissy walking toward the stairs.

"Nothing's wrong. It's just . . . I told you I wanted to find out what happened to my parents. So I've got things to do."

"That shouldn't keep us apart all day," he said quietly.

She couldn't tell him what she'd overheard, especially since Cissy was coming down the hall. And she wouldn't tell him anyway, ever. It was too humiliating.

"I appreciate your thinking of me. Perhaps another day." She didn't miss the curious glance Cissy gave her as she passed. Leah looked down at the telephone table.

"I see," Merrick said heavily. "I'll talk to you later, then."

When he'd cut the connection, she stood there for several moments, holding the receiver tightly. Then she replaced it.

Cissy called back brightly, "If you don't have any plans, Leah, let's take a ride this afternoon."

She tried to demur. "I don't have any clothes or boots."

"Don't worry. I've found some things. Lilac will bring them to your room."

The morning seemed interminable. Leah walked restlessly around and out into the gardens. She wondered if she should pack her things and drive off.

But that would delight John Edward and Cissy, wouldn't it? They wanted her to drop her questions, to leave everything as it had been—murky and secret. And what about her grandmother? Carrie would not be pleased at all.

Despite the pain she felt, she wasn't going to go until she succeeded in learning the truth about her parents. She wouldn't let anyone or anything drive her away. Not even a bruised and disillusioned heart.

Perhaps Kent Ellis had made some discoveries. Leah hurried across the footbridge, passed the clearing and plunged into the forest of immense trees. She found Kent kneeling beside one of the slave cabins, carefully easing what looked like pieces of dirty chalk from the surrounding dirt.

"Bones," he explained briefly. Then he rocked back on his heels. " 'Morning, Leah. How are you?"

" 'Morning, Kent. Fine." Would she ever mean it again? The pain of her disappointment in Merrick made her feel old and somber. She forced a smile. "How about you? Any more close calls?"

He didn't smile in return. "Not yet." His mouth looked tight and hard. "I'm being very careful." He stood up and brushed off his Levi's. "I've been nosing around, and I think there's a real story about what happened to your parents."

"Kent, what have you found out?"

"Not one thing that's concrete, but I talked to Lilac and she's scared to death. She knows something."

"I'll go see her," Leah said excitedly.

"Wait up, Leah. She's not going to say any more. Jason's your best bet. Go see him in the hospital. He'll talk."

All the way back to the house, Leah rehearsed it in her mind. As soon as she returned from her ride with Cissy, she'd call the hospital and find out the visiting hours.

Cissy greeted her on the back steps. "Leah, I've been looking for you. Aunt Carrie's ready to lunch with us."

In the cool dimness of the second-story veranda, they had a fruit salad of strawberries, cantaloupe, grapes, raspberries, watermelon and bananas, and a frosted lime drink.

Lunch was lighthearted and interesting, with Carrie regaling Leah and Cissy with stories of her many adventures in Nice. After lunch, Carrie excused herself to take a rest. It was then that the tone of the afternoon changed.

"I'll meet you at the stables in fifteen minutes," Cissy said.

"I don't imagine I can wear your things."

"I found some of your mother's riding clothes in the attic. I'm sure they'll fit."

The clothes were waiting on her bed, tan jodhpurs and a white shirt, freshly laundered. Well-worn leather boots sat on the floor. Leah could smell the polish that had been used on them. Reluctantly, she picked up the shirt.

The clothes did fit. And so did the boots.

She looked in the mirror and knew her mother must have stood there often, wearing these clothes. Mary Ellen had seen the image Leah now saw. And before them had been Marthe, small and dark with a quicksilver quality, not quite definite and clear, too elusive to capture.

Leah didn't like the way she felt as she walked down the back veranda steps. It was as if she weren't herself alone, as if she carried other personalities with her. She wished she hadn't agreed to wear these clothes or take the ride. She stopped halfway to the stables and almost turned back, but Cissy came out of the tack room just then and called to her.

The breeze was sharpening to a wind. Gray clouds dulled the sky, hiding the sun. It wasn't a very nice day for a ride. But she went obediently down the path.

The horses were ready, Cissy's a piebald, Leah's a fidgety black mare.

The stableboy came out and said, "Granddaddy wanted me to tell you, Miss Cissy, there's a tropical storm watch."

"Thank you, Bobby. I heard the forecast, too. Nothing's expected to come inland until late tomorrow."

So they mounted, though the wind was high enough now to rattle loose shingles on the stable roof and kick up a little dust devil in the beaten ground of the bridle path.

Cissy had to speak loudly for Leah to hear her. "We'll go that way." She pointed to a trail that curved into the pines. "There's an old picnic place there. It's a nice ride." With that she was off.

Leah nudged her horse and cantered along behind. Cissy sat a horse well, her back as straight as a rod. She looked around once or twice, and when they came out of the pines onto a dirt road, she called, "Shall we?" At Leah's nod, they urged their horses to a gallop and rode hard and fast for almost a mile.

As they gradually slowed and eased into a walk, Leah came up beside her. "Are we almost there?"

"About a quarter mile more. We used to ride here when we were kids, John Edward and Mary Ellen and I, with Merrick tagging along. Old Jason came with us, telling us what to do, especially Mary Ellen, who used to yank the reins all the time."

Leah looked up the dusty road, trying to visualize an uneven group of riders with a slim, dark girl always in a hurry. But the road lay empty, gloomy with the huge pines tossing in the wind and the pewter-colored sky pressing close to the earth.

Cissy urged her horse to a trot, and Leah kept pace. The road curved away, but they cut off, following a faint path. They went slowly now, stepping over broken branches, once skirting a fallen palm. The trees closed in overhead, blocking out the light. On a hot, sunny day, the area would have been refreshing, but the high whine of the wind and the heavy air made it somber and cheerless.

The path twisted among the trees, dropping steadily, coming out finally in an overgrown clearing. Once, years ago, it must have been a beautiful spot, tranquil and sheltered, an airy retreat from the summer heat. Two rough-hewn wooden tables, shaded by a huge live oak, looked out over a broad sweep of river; but lightning had struck the oak, and a huge branch had crashed down to shatter one table. Thick, waist-high grass undulated in the sharp wind off the gray water like underwater tendrils of swamp grass.

Cissy turned a little in her saddle. They faced each other, and Leah realized they were adversaries, if not enemies.

"I had to talk to you," Cissy said almost stridently.

Leah stared at her, waiting.

"I'm going to tell you what happened to your parents."

Leah heart began to thud. Whatever she had expected, it wasn't this.

"I want you to understand that I'd give anything not to have to tell you this." Cissy paused. "I'd give almost anything—but not Aunt Carrie's happiness or peace of mind. I've thought about it and thought about it. If Aunt Carrie learned the truth, it would kill her."

Leah's hands tightened on the reins, and her horse shifted uneasily.

"Look, didn't Louisa tell you anything?"

"No."

"Nothing at all?"

"Nothing."

Cissy bit her lip and frowned.

"What are you trying to tell me?" Leah's voice sounded thin and defensive.

Cissy looked at Leah, her face smooth and lovely, her brilliant red hair sleek in spite of the whip of the wind. "Mary Ellen shot Tom, then shot herself." She said it quietly, almost matter-of-factly.

"No." It was a whisper, full of pain and heartbreak.

"I'm sorry, Leah. I didn't want you to know. No one wanted you to know. But don't you see what you've done by coming here? Aunt Carrie may begin to wonder if they did go down on The New Star. If you keep on poking and prodding, she'll begin to consider what might have happened. Then, if she really remembers the way Mary Ellen was, she'll soon realize what must have happened."

"How do you know what happened?" Leah demanded.

"Don't you think it might be better just to leave it like this and never speak of it again? It won't help if you—"

"No! I must know—I must!"

Cissy stared out at the heaving gray water, then shrugged. "They quarreled soon after they arrived. Obviously, as things turned out, that quarrel was more serious than we thought. He must have had his suspicions . . ."

"What are you talking about?"

Cissy stared at her, green eyes cool and unfriendly. "Mary Ellen always wanted what she couldn't have, even as a little girl. Usually, one way or another, she got what she wanted. She used to tease us when we were little and say that she was really Marthe, that she lived in Marthe's room and that Marthe had always done what she wanted and the devil take the hindmost. Sometimes I thought she was possessed—then again, I would know she was riding us, one more way of making it clear that she was really a Devereaux and we weren't, that she looked like Marthe and we didn't."

Cissy's voice throbbed with anger. How she must have hated Mary Ellen. After all these years, she hated her still.

A pulse moved in her throat. "It must have been the same old story. Mary Ellen got Tom, then decided she didn't want him, that she really wanted John Edward. Of course, Aunt Carrie wouldn't have put up with that for a minute. 'You've made your bed, now you lie in it,' that's what Aunt Carrie would've said. Maybe she told Tom she was through with him and was going to stay at Devereaux Plantation. Then they quarreled, and when he tried to make her go back to the boat, she shot him. When she realized what she'd done, she took the gun and—"

"You don't know that," Leah interrupted. "You don't know any of it. You're making it up."

Cissy stared at her blankly, her face chalk-white. Gradually, reason came back into her eyes. "You must understand," she said quietly, "I'm trying to help you. I don't know what really happened. But it must have been something like that, because I know what I saw."

It was darker now in the isolated glade on the riverbank, the clouds thickening. Cissy's face was indistinct in the gloom.

"Louisa came running up from . . . from the boat. It was almost night by then and raining hard. I had just come in from checking the stables and still wore my raincoat. She was very upset, but she wouldn't say what was wrong. She just begged me to come with her to the boat." Cissy glanced toward the river. "You can almost see the dock from here."

Leah could barely distinguish the weathered pilings from the gray, wind-tossed water.

"I ran down the path with her. She was hysterical . . ."

Leah looked at Cissy sharply. She couldn't imagine Louisa Shaw ever being hysterical.

". . . and I understood why when we reached the boat. Mary Ellen and Tom were in the main cabin—dead. Tom was lying on his back. Mary Ellen had fallen across him. I didn't see her face, but the back of her head was gone."

Leah made a small sound.

"I'm sorry," Cissy said quickly. But Leah knew she wasn't sorry, no matter what she might say, now or in the future.

"I ran and fetched Jason. We could trust Jason."

"What did you do?"

"Your grandmother begged me to help her get rid of the bodies. She was afraid it would be too devastating for you if it all came out. Of course, it would have been awful, with the newspapers dragging up everything about Marthe. The press would have had a field day."

Leah nodded slowly. She could see how that would be true.

So they'd worked hard and fast, though hampered by the wind and the rain, and had wrapped the bodies. It was easier for Leah to think of them like that, not as her parents, not as Mary Ellen and Tom, but as bodies, inert, unfeeling, weighted with chains found God knew where by Jason and dumped into the wild, high-flowing river to be swept out to sea. Finally, Cissy and Jason had stood in the rain and watched the lights of The New Star fade into nothingness.

"None of it need ever have happened," Cissy said bitterly. "It was all Mary Ellen's fault."

CHAPTER THIRTEEN

Leah wheeled her horse around. Ignoring Cissy's call, she urged the mare along the faint trail, slowing only where fallen branches blocked the way. When she reached the dirt road, she gave the mare her head and rode like the wind, but the thunder of the horse's hooves only echoed that devastating refrain, "Mary Ellen's fault, Mary Ellen's fault, Mary Ellen's fault."

Bobby heard the hoofbeats and ran out of the stables, alarmed.

Leah swung to the ground and tossed him the reins, ignoring the question in his face. She hurried up the oyster-shell path. She couldn't talk to anyone right now.

The huge pines bent beneath the rising wind. The creak of their branches mingled with the shrill cries of the sea gulls. The wind keened through loose boards in the dilapidated tower.

She slowed a little and stared up at the house. It looked smaller in the heavy gray air, pulled in upon itself, withdrawn. Her room was on the northwest side. Her room. Mary Ellen's room. Marthe's room.

As she watched, she saw Henry come around the corner of the second-story veranda and begin to struggle with the shutters on that side. He was battening down Devereaux Plantation for another storm. The house had withstood storms for almost three centuries.

Three centuries. So many lives had been played out in that house and on those broad verandas. And somewhere in that line of forceful people who had withstood Indians, plagues, war and famine, did there run a strain of darkness, a selfish, twisted refusal to be thwarted no matter what the cost?

Was that her legacy?

The path turned her, and she faced directly into the wind. She had to lean into it and struggle to move forward. She had grown up with the wind that could shatter concrete buildings, uproot steel, topple brick walls. She understood that kind of wind. She knew, too, the wind that came before a spring rain, blowing one way, then another. But she didn't know a wind that came hard and flat and steadily from one direction. The sky was still a smoky, sullen pewter color, but there were no mountainous banks of purplish-black thunderclouds, like those that hung in a tornadic Texas sky. She battled the wind and was grateful to reach the lee of the house.

She looked swiftly around but saw no one. Relieved, she hurried up the rear steps to the second-floor veranda, hesitating for a moment when she reached the screen door to her room.

Her room. Mary Ellen's room. Marthe's room.

Then she plunged inside, closed the door and turned on the light. Once again, she looked at her image in the mirror. A white face, windblown hair and huge dark eyes stared back at her.

"I should never have come."

She said it aloud, to that forlorn image in the mirror, to a wounded heart.

Grandmother Shaw had left everything she'd known behind her, a middle-aged woman fleeing a horror too great to be borne.

Leah slumped onto the dressing-table chair. In Louisa's letter, she'd said she was wrong about that night . . .

Wrong about what? Leah sat bolt upright. Wrong that Mary Ellen had killed her husband and then herself? How had Louisa been deceived? And by whom? Color surged into Leah's face.

Cissy said that Louisa had come running to the house to get help. That could be true enough. If Louisa had found Mary Ellen and Tom dead, could someone have convinced her it was murder and suicide when it was really murder and murder?

It was all linked to the appearance of the ghost. Or was it?

Leah got up and paced wearily up and down. She could imagine and guess and hope, but there was no way she could ever know. . . . Her pacing slowed. There was still one person alive who knew something of what had actually happened—Old Jason. He'd told Kent that Mary Ellen haunted him, lying in that cursed ground.

Leah frowned. Mary Ellen and Tom had been thrown into the river. Jason must have confused Mary Ellen with Marthe, who was buried in unhallowed ground.

She pressed her hands to her temples and closed her eyes tight. Marthe and Mary Ellen. Mary Ellen and Marthe. And her.

She stood in the middle of the room, trembling; then gradually, unexpectedly, a feeling of calm filled her. Louisa and Cissy could have been wrong. She wasn't going to give up on that. At least not until she'd talked to Jason.

She glanced at her watch. It was just past four. Perhaps she could—Lightning crackled, and suddenly rain swept against the house in blinding sheets. She walked to the window and peered out. No, she wouldn't be driving into Mefford today. But she could call the hospital, find out what the visiting hours were and go see him tomorrow.

She hurried downstairs to the telephone in the alcove near the main staircase. It took a few minutes to find the number, then explain who she was to the hospital operator and that she wanted to visit Old Jason from Devereaux Plantation.

The hospital operator knew his name and apparently knew of her. "Oh, he'll be so pleased, Miss Shaw. You can come in the morning. And he's doing very well. He's old, of course, but he's gaining strength. He'll be so happy to have someone from the plantation visit him."

Leah was putting down the receiver when she heard the front door open. She turned and saw Merrick standing there, his face grim and hard. "I called you. All afternoon."

"I took a ride with Cissy." She could see pain in his eyes, as she had when they'd walked in the garden at Ashwood and he'd told her about his marriage and waited for her response.

But that was all fake, wasn't it? He didn't love her. He loved Ashwood and would do whatever was necessary to make certain that he would inherit it, just as Cissy and John Edward intended to stay always at Devereaux House.

"Ashwood is one of the Devereaux plantations, isn't it?" she said bluntly.

"Yes, it is. Why?"

"You oversee all of them for Grandmother."

"Yes. Yes, I do."

She started to turn away.

He reached out and pulled her around to face him. "Dammit, what's wrong with you?"

She stood frozen, then said huskily, "It's just . . . I believed it, you know. I thought it was like a fairy tale. But I should have known better."

"Known what?" His face was heavy with anger.

"You don't really care for me. It's only Ashwood you love."

"Who's been talking to you?" he demanded.

"No one." She fought back tears. "But I overheard Cissy and John Edward. They think it's wonderful, the way you've persuaded me to believe that you care. They're so pleased. I'm sure they think that will make it so much easier for all of you to remain in control of Grandmother's properties."

His hand fell away from her, and he stepped back a pace. "How could you . . ." He stared at her, his eyes stricken. "How could you believe that?"

She clenched her hands tightly. "What else can I believe?"

"A great many things," he said in a bitter voice. "If you loved me, you would believe in me—not them!" He turned around and strode off.

She watched as the front door slammed shut behind him. She stood still for a long moment, her heart aching; then she ran to the door and opened it, just in time to see the station wagon jolt out of the driveway.

But that was better, wasn't it? She shouldn't try to talk to him again. Her mind must control her heart.

"Leah." John Edward stood behind her in the doorway to the library. "Do you have a moment?"

She turned and saw a middle-aged man with a boyish face and

hostile eyes. He was so irrelevant to the feelings of loss and pain that swirled within her.

He stepped out into the hallway, and the light from the chandeliers made his hair glisten like gold. "I need to talk to you." His manner was determined and not especially pleasant.

"Of course, John Edward." She walked into the library, and he followed, closing the door behind them. They faced each other, hostility crackling in the room.

He jammed his hands into his pockets. "It's pretty clear what you're up to."

"What do you mean?" Her voice was as hard as his.

His mouth twisted in a humorless smile. "Little Miss Innocence, aren't you? Carrying ugly tales to an old lady with a heart condition."

"She had a right to know what's happening."

"Even if it kills her?"

Sudden fear shot through Leah. Had something happened to her grandmother? She turned to reach for the door.

John Edward caught her by the wrist. "Oh, no, you're not going to bother her again. She had an attack of angina this afternoon, but she took a nitroglycerin tablet and it passed. She's asleep now."

"She was fine at lunch," Leah said loudly.

"Maybe. All I know is she's sick now. And we know who's telling her lies."

"Not lies. The truth."

"Does it matter, if it kills her?" He stared, his eyes cold. "But that's what you want, isn't it?"

"No! That's terrible—"

"Then you can inherit Devereaux Plantation."

"I don't want Devereaux Plantation!" Leah was close to tears. She pulled away from him and opened the door.

"Don't you?" he called after her.

Leah ran up the stairs. Why hadn't they told her that Carrie was ill? She felt isolated, a pariah. She turned toward her grandmother's room and knocked lightly on the door.

Cissy opened the door, her face pale and set. She still wore her riding clothes. She stepped out into the hall and stared at Leah. "She's sleeping. Haven't you done enough?"

Tears swam in Leah's eyes.

"Why don't you get out?" Cissy demanded in a low harsh voice. "Leave us alone. We were fine until you came."

"I suppose you were," Leah said miserably, aware of the anger stirring within her. It wasn't she who had staged a ghostly appearance in the garden or had arranged accidents. "But I'm not going until I learn the truth about my mother—until I talk to Old Jason and find out what really happened that night."

She turned away and hurried to the sanctuary of her room. At dinnertime, she sent word that she would have a tray in her room. She checked twice on her grandmother, who once roused enough to smile warmly at her.

But as the storm ebbed and rose, rain sometimes rattling the windows, sometimes easing softly against the panes, Leah sat in her room and remembered Merrick's face and how the anguish in his eyes had turned to bitterness.

She also remembered what Cissy and John Edward had said. Somehow she would survive the pain in her foolish heart.

Finally, after the house had settled into quietness, she decided to take advantage of a lull in the storm. She pulled on a sweater and walked along the veranda and down the steps into the garden. She ambled toward the pond, but she knew no ghosts would be out on a night like this. The trees still whipped, and thunder rumbled ominously. The storm wasn't over.

As she came back up the path amid a burst of rain slanting in from the southeast, she realized it was on a night such as this that her parents had died.

When she reached the steps, she paused and looked down toward the pond. She could almost picture Louisa running up the path, frightened and horrified. The idea was so unbearable to Leah that she began to run up the steps in an effort to block it out. Just then a rush of air fanned her, and the earth next to her shuddered.

Her hand flew to her throat as she stared down at a broken jumble of pottery and huge clumps of earth. An immense urn that sat on the second-story veranda had crashed to the ground at the very spot where she had been standing. If she hadn't moved when she had, the falling urn would have crushed her. Slowly, horror welled inside her. She looked up, but nothing moved on the second story.

Her heart thudded erratically, she began again to climb the stairs. She moved cautiously, trying to see into the darker shadows. Once she had reached her room and opened the screen door, she turned on the lamp and looked in every corner. Satisfied she was alone, she locked the veranda door and pushed a chair beneath the knob to the hall door.

Gradually, her breathing eased, though she still looked nervously from one door to the other whenever the wind rattled the old house.

But the killer who moved so quietly under cover of night specialized in seeming accidents. A tumbling wall, a boat swept away, a broken well ladder. Now a falling urn that weighed, perhaps, a hundred pounds.

If she hadn't moved unexpectedly, she would be dead.

She clasped her hands together so hard they ached. A monstrous thought ballooned in her mind, ugly as a malignant growth. Nothing had threatened her until she and Merrick had quarreled.

When she'd come to Devereaux Plantation and been taken into the family, everyone knew that, though Carrie Devereaux would be generous to her adopted niece and nephews, Devereaux Plantation would ultimately come to Leah. And the other plantations, too. Including Ashwood.

Leah moved like an old woman. She slipped into her nightgown and settled in the high bed. She lay in darkness, listening to the whine of the wind, and resolved to talk to Old Jason tomorrow. She would do that much more. Then she would tell Carrie that she had to be getting back to Texas; she would visit, of course, and write, but she wouldn't live at Devereaux Plantation. She wasn't going to stay in this house with its record of twisted lives and broken dreams.

Leah slept fitfully, awakening once to look about in terror, her heart racing, sure that someone had called out. But it was only the wind.

MIDNIGHT, SATURDAY, MAY 9,1863

Marthe knelt in the darkness, her fingers reaching beneath the bed for the valise. Where was it? It had to be there. Then she touched its petit-point cover and found the smooth leather handles. Feverishly, she unbuckled the clasp and shoved the family Bible in on top of her few pieces of clothing. She hadn't intended to take the Bible, not until that last awful scene with Randolph, but now she would. And she had already inked in—indelibly for all time—her name and Timothy's in the marriage column at the front, for they would be married as soon as possible. Timothy had sent word that he would arrange it. A momentary feeling of panic swept over her. Timothy seemed so far away, and she couldn't quite see his face. Oh, her mother would have been so heartbroken if she had lived to see this day—Marthe driven from her own home, creeping through the night like a loose woman to meet a man and ride away with him under cover of dark.Marthe buckled the clasp, picked up the valise and tiptoed to the screen door. She edged it open, then slipped outside. The moonlight was bright, but just then a cloud slid across the moon. Welcoming the darkness, Marthe crept toward the stairs, on her way to the tower.

CHAPTER FOURTEEN

Carrie Devereaux sent for Leah shortly after breakfast.

Leah found her propped up in bed, three down pillows behind her, her face pale. She held a writing board in her lap and waved Leah to a seat beside her. As she started to talk, a faint flush brightened her cheeks, and her black eyes sparkled.

"We must introduce you to our friends and to other members of the family—cousins and second cousins. There is so much to be done. I'm trying to decide on a time."

"Grandmother," Leah cautioned, "you mustn't talk so fast. You must rest."

Carrie's eyes glittered. "Now, don't you start that nonsense with me. John Edward and Cissy have gloomed around, wringing their hands. I've had angina for forty years." She laughed grimly. "I don't suppose I'll have it for forty more, but I don't spend a half minute worrying about it, and you're not going to, either." She rattled her papers. "I've started some lists. The ballroom on the third floor must be repainted. And we'll have a fine dinner. The servants must start preparing now. Everything must be polished and . . ."

The night before, Leah had resolved to leave after speaking to Jason. This morning, watching a pulse flutter in her grandmother's throat, listening to her excited chatter about future plans, she made a new resolve. She wouldn't be driven away from Devereaux Plantation. If she left, it would wound a heart that had already borne more than its share of suffering.

No matter what she learned from Jason, she wouldn't let it drive her away. She still feared there was a link, a thread of tragedy, running from Marthe to Mary Ellen to herself, but whatever happened, she would manage. She would not become hysterical.

Merrick came in then. "Good morning, Aunt Carrie," he said softly. He nodded stiffly at Leah. Crossing to the bed, he bent to bestow a light kiss on Carrie's cheek. That simple gesture told Leah he loved her grandmother. When he straightened, he looked down at the old woman, his face somber, and both she and Leah realized something was wrong.

"What is it, Merrick?" Carrie asked sharply.

"Old Jason died last night."

Carrie took a deep breath, turned her face away for an instant, then looked back at them. Leah ached for her. She was old and knew she was old, and any death presaged her own. But she spoke calmly. "Was anyone with him at the end? Did they call Henry?"

Merrick shook his head. "No. Henry told me this morning that he went to see him last night and Jason was fine. He was looking forward to seeing Leah this morning. He died in his sleep."

For the first time, Leah realized that Henry was Jason's son. She thought again how interwoven and tangled were all the lives at Devereaux Plantation.

Carrie Devereaux looked past them, beyond them. "I came to Devereaux Plantation in 1938 as a bride. Old Jason was the butler. He must have been well past forty then. We depended upon him. He was part of us. It was Jason who roused us the night the fire broke out in the kitchen. That was in 1946. He and my husband, Samuel, fought the fire and saved Devereaux Plantation. And many years later it was Jason who brought us word that Samuel's brother and his wife had died, so we invited Cissy, John Edward and Merrick to live with us. After Samuel died, Jason was always there, helping me with the children, keeping things going. It was Jason—" now she spoke so softly they had to strain to hear "—who found Mary Ellen's charm bracelet on the path near the tower and brought it to me with tears in his eyes."

She reached over to the table beside the bed and picked up a small teakwood box carved with dragons and swallows. Opening it, she lifted out a fine-linked silver bracelet. The tiny charms struck against one another, making a faint and ghostly melody.

Leah stared at the bracelet and felt the blood leave her face. Her mother's bracelet. She wanted to shake her head. No, Jason hadn't found it on the path. It hadn't been that way at all. He had unclasped that bracelet from an unfeeling arm to give Carrie Devereaux the only thing he could give her of her daughter. If ever Leah had wanted proof that Old Jason knew more of what had happened to her mother and father, this silver bracelet was it.

Leah's grandmother handed the bracelet to her. She touched each charm in turn—a horse, a deer, the initials M.E. worked together, a train car, a sailboat. Each one would have meant something special to Mary Ellen. To Leah, they represented the reality of her search and at the same time its futility—because Old Jason was dead. She couldn't ask him what had happened that stormy night.

Carrie was still looking at the bracelet, not at her. Leah knew her face must have revealed something of her shock and despair because Merrick was watching her with a thoughtful frown.

Carrie took the bracelet back and held it tightly. "Mary Ellen's gone, and now Old Jason." She sighed tiredly. "Merrick, will you see to everything?"

"Of course."

She pushed aside the writing board and the sheets of paper covered with her small, fine handwriting. "I'll rest now," she said.

They left her there, still holding the silver bracelet and looking at a past they couldn't see.

As they came out into the hall, Henry was turning away from the telephone alcove.

Leah could see the grief and pain in his face. "Henry, I'm so sorry . . ."

"Miss Leah, Mr. Merrick." Henry's voice was high with shock. "The sheriff just called me. He said . . ."

Leah knew without even hearing Henry's words. She thought of the tumbling wall and the cut anchor rope, the sabotaged ladder and the falling urn, and she knew.

"... with a pillow." Henry stopped speaking, and tears brimmed from his eyes. "Smothered him with a pillow." He turned and stumbled away from them, his grief for an aging father turned to horror.

It was cool and quiet, eerily quiet, in the upper hallway, cool and dark and somber as the rain pelted against the windows.

"It's my fault," Leah said faintly. "Oh, my God, it's my fault."

Merrick gripped her arms. "Your fault? What are you talking about?"

"I called the hospital," she said dully. "I called and said I was going to visit Jason this morning."

His hands fell away from her, but his frown remained. "Why should someone kill Jason because you were going to see him?"

"Jason knew what really happened to my mother and father. He helped get rid of their bodies."

Merrick stood so still he might have been carved from stone. Then he asked, his voice harsh, "Leah, what are you talking about?"

She told him then of Cissy's story.

"Cissy told you that she and Jason helped your grandmother Shaw dispose of Mary Ellen and Tom?" There was a horrified incredulity in his voice.

"You didn't know?"

"Of course not! And I can't imagine Cissy ..."

Cissy was so elegant and aloof and dignified. It was hard to picture her running through the rain, struggling to hide a scandal to protect Leah.

"Cissy never gave enough of a damn about anybody to go to that kind of trouble. Nobody but Hal, that is. And she wasn't married to him then." He paused, his eyes narrowed. "Oh. Hal. Of course. That's why she helped Louisa."

"What did Hal have to do with any of it?"

"Cissy and Hal." There was an odd tone in Merrick's voice. "God knows, a lot of marriages aren't made in heaven." His mouth twisted a little. "That I can testify to. But Cissy and Hal . . . They're so damned unlikely for a great love match, yet that's what it is. Cissy had an almost unholy passion for that guy, wet fish that he is. She always did. And that was just about the time he must have been ready to propose. She wouldn't have wanted any nasty scandals marring his picture of the Devereaux. Hal was probably going to some lengths to overlook the ancient trouble about Marthe. He's as nutty about family stuff as anybody in the county. It would have meant everything to Cissy to keep it all quiet.

"So I suppose," he said slowly, "that what she told you could be true."

Leah shook her head violently. "No, it wasn't right! Not the part about my mother killing my father."

"Why do you say that?"

"Don't you see? Jason's murder proves that someone did kill my parents. Jason knew it—and the murderer couldn't take the chance that he'd tell me."

The murderer.

It could have been Cissy. Or she might be an innocent party, knowing only what she saw and becoming part of a conspiracy to protect her future with Hal.

It could have been John Edward, angry over his loss of Mary Ellen.

Merrick could have known and helped keep it quiet; he could be willing now to go to any length to keep it that way.

Leah stepped back from him, her hand going up to her throat.

The silence expanded between them.

Finally, icily, he said, "You're very transparent, Leah." He looked at her a moment longer, then walked away. At the top of the stairs he paused to look back at her. "And very dramatic. But a little hysterical. It's odd, having someone think you are a maniac. It's certainly not very flattering."

Leah watched him leave and still she stood there, her hand at her throat. Was she hysterical?

Old Jason was dead, murdered.

The night before, an urn had fallen from the second-story veranda to crash on the spot she'd just vacated.

Leah went back to her room. Once again, she locked both doors. The house seemed to emanate danger. Murder walked at Devereaux Plantation.

Was the killer Merrick?

She didn't want to believe that. He'd only been a boy when her parents had died. But greed knew no age. Was his passion for Ashwood evidence of a reverence of things old and lovely? Or was it the fruit of an overweening greed to possess?

Not Merrick. Please, not Merrick.

But she remembered his eyes, cold and hostile now, eyes in which she'd once seen—or imagined—a flame of love.

Would Cissy protect him?

Yes, if it were to her benefit. She would do anything to protect the Devereaux name from scandal and keep safe her romance with Hal. Equally, of course, she would have protected John Edward, and for the same reasons. The story she'd told could have been the truth—twisted about. Perhaps John Edward had continued to want Mary Ellen and tried to persuade her to leave Tom. Then, when he'd been rebuffed, he'd killed her in a surge of rage. Then he'd killed Tom to cover up his crime and called on Cissy to help him. She could have taken that truth and twisted it to make Mary Ellen the pursuer and so convince a distraught Louisa Shaw. After all, Louisa barely knew her daughter-in-law, and to have Mary Ellen's own cousins describe her as fickle and dangerous . . .

Leah nodded. She could see how it might have happened that way. But, despite her fear and uncertainty, she felt the beginning of a great exultation. Her mother had not killed her father. The rain could spatter against her windows, the lowering skies could press darkly down, death could walk in the night—but nothing daunted her now. Mary Ellen's image moved in her mind, small and slight, lively, clever and loving; not a driven, twisted creature doomed to reenact Marthe's deadly role.

Louisa Shaw had been right. There was great evil at Devereaux Plantation.

Leah paced up and down, stopping occasionally to listen to the storm. The rain was coming down even harder now. If only she had gone into Mefford yesterday afternoon and talked to Old Jason. Kent Ellis had talked to Lilac and come away certain she knew more than she would admit.

Lilac. She, too, had been at Devereaux Plantation when the murders took place. What did she know?

Leah went out into the hall and used the phone to call the kitchen.

"No, ma'am," a subdued voice told her. "Lilac, she got sick and went to her room."

Leah replaced the receiver and returned to her room. Lilac would have heard of Jason's murder. Could fear have driven her to her bed?

Lightning split the rain-riven sky, bathing the landscape in a sulfurish light. In the brief flash, Leah saw the servants' quarters. She whirled around to the closet and yanked out her raincoat, then stepped out onto the veranda and paused, momentarily dismayed by the force of the storm. She pulled a scarf out of her pocket and tucked it around her head. Then, turning up the collar of her coat, she hurried to the back steps and paused once more before plunging into the rain.

She ran, head down, splashing through pools dotting on the oyster-shell path. The wind rattled the palms while the rain battered the roses. The rain seeped through her coat, plastering her scarf to her head.

Leah felt a wave of relief when she reached the servants' quarters. The violence of the storm frightened her more than she wanted to admit. She knocked on the door and saw a light glowing behind closed white curtains. She knocked louder, thinking she couldn't be heard over the roar of the storm. Finally, the door was opened a narrow space. Leah pulled at the screen door, but it was latched.

"What is it?"

"Lilac, I have to talk to you."

Leah heard her breathing quickly behind the nearly closed door. The woman said nothing at all.

"Lilac, you've got to tell me what happened to my parents. You know—"

"I don't know nothin'. Not nothing Miss Leah, and don't you go 'round sayin' I do. And I don't want to talk to you." She paused, then whispered, "Get you back to Texas, miss," and slammed the door.

Leah shivered, but the cold that touched her bones came from within, not from the rain. Lilac knew, but she would never admit it.

Fear gripped Leah. She was alone with no one to trust. And death moved under cover of the Carolina nights.

She turned and started back up the path. Gusts of rain swept in silvery sheets against the house. Somehow the building looked insubstantial and ghostlike—and frightening. Abruptly, she swerved around and headed down the path.

The water overflowed the banks of the pond, lapping close to the footbridge. If the storm continued, the bridge would soon be awash. Leah hurried across and pushed her way through the whipping fronds of the willows. She followed the path and welcomed the protection of the huge pines. It was almost calm in the thick wood, though it was hard to see through the dank green gloom. At the top of the hill, as she left the protection of the trees and moved into the full force of the storm, it occurred to her to wonder whether she would find Kent Ellis. Surely he would have taken shelter somewhere. But she was so near that she continued on and found Kent snug in his tent.

He folded up his low camp table, making room for her, gave her a blanket to wrap herself up in and poured her a cup of coffee from his thermos.

As she drank, she told him about Old Jason.

"I'll be damned." Kent looked at her soberly. "You'd better be careful."

She shivered, though the blanket was warm. Rain slapped against the tent sides. "I will." Then she told him how she'd tried to talk to Lilac.

"I didn't get anything definite out of her, either," he said. "The only thing I'm certain about is that she does know something—and she's scared to death of it. Which shows she isn't stupid. All she did was mutter about Miss Marthe."

Marthe. Everything seemed to go back to her and to the ghost named after her. Everything . . . Leah felt a tingle of excitement. Everything went back to the appearances of the ghost. The Whispering Lady had appeared, and Carrie had almost died. The ghost had come back this summer, and Kent . . .

Why Kent?

Leah leaned forward. "What did you do the week before the chimney fell on you?"

Kent looked at her blankly.

"Here on the plantation," she said impatiently. "What were you doing?"

"Oh. Yeah. Just a minute." He reached beneath his cot and dragged out a metal filing box, opened it, searched for a minute, then took out a yellow spiral notebook. "That would be the first week in June," he muttered to himself. He flipped some pages over and handed the notebook to her. "Here."

He had kept a daily record of his work. She began to read; the only sounds were the rustle of the pages and the steady beat of the rain against the canvas tent. One entry she read and reread: "June 3. Circled tower. Door locked. Looks sturdy. Interesting to see interior, but not likely. J.E.D. found me shaking the lock and told me to keep away from the place, said it was dangerous. Doesn't look dangerous. Well site looks . . ."

J.E.D. John Edward Devereaux. He'd warned Kent to keep away from the tower, and a few days later the ghost had appeared and Kent's accidents had begun.

Old Jason had told Carrie he'd found Mary Ellen's bracelet near the tower.

The tower was the only place on Devereaux Plantation that was closed and locked.

Leah shivered.

"Still cold? Want some more coffee?" Kent asked.

She drank another cup, looked a little further in the notebook, then handed it back.

"You didn't find anything?"

She almost told him. But she had called Mefford Hospital, and an old man had died. If she told Kent, he would want to force their way into the tower now, to see what was there. She wasn't going to put anyone else in danger.

After thanking him for the coffee, Leah started back and was drenched again before she'd taken more than a dozen steps. She struggled through the garden; then, halfway back to the house, took the path leading to the stables and the garage.

The wind was blowing harder. Leah leaned into it, the rain enveloping her. She was almost to the garage when she heard the low, throaty roar of a sports car. She stepped off the path and pressed close to the rough-edged trunk of a palmetto.

John Edward's yellow Porsche swept up the driveway.

She waited until John Edward had got out of the car and disappeared in the rain before she cautiously approached the garage. Slipping inside, she checked the cars. She knew them now—John Edward's Porsche, Merrick's battered station wagon, Cissy's Mercedes, Carrie's Cadillac and, of course, her own rented Vega.

Leah peered through a dusty side window. The tower stood just past the garage, dark and menacing. Lightning flashed again, illuminating the windows at the top.

If she could find a flashlight and something to break the chain . . .

The tack room held tools and several flashlights. She grabbed up a wire cutter, a hatchet and a crowbar. Then she saw the oil lanterns in the corner. They would be needed, of course, when storms downed the electrical lines. Leah found a can of kerosene and poured some into a lantern.

She ducked her head against the swirling rain as she hurried up the path, clutching her awkward load. At the tower door she paused, feeling a sweep of revulsion. She didn't really want to probe the old building, because she was almost certain she knew what it hid. Jason told her grandmother that he'd found Mary Ellen's bracelet near the tower. Years later, he babbled that Mary Ellen haunted him because she was buried in unhallowed ground. He hadn't made a mistake. He hadn't meant Marthe. He'd meant Mary Ellen, just as he'd said.

Grim-faced, she took the wire cutters, clamped them on the chain and pressed. With a sharp clank, the chain gave way and clattered against the door.

Leah looked nervously around. Rain still swept down in a thin gray sheet, almost obscuring the stables and the garage. Palmettos rattled. Live oak limbs swayed and creaked. But no one moved in the wild wetness.

Leah pulled the loose chain out of the hasp and turned the door handle. The door moved easily, and that surprised her. It had been closed for so many years, yet it swung open smoothly and quietly.

Stepping inside, she closed the door behind her, then used the flashlight to illuminate the lantern. She knelt and lit it, and a sharp smell of kerosene overlay the dank odor of the tower. The flame danced up the wick, throwing a bright circle of orange light. She set the lamp carefully to one side and glanced around.

Her first thought was that the place was very small. Then she looked up, following the spiral of steps that disappeared into the darkness above. Light from the lantern flickered unevenly, throwing her shadow against the angled walls, and she realized with a start that this was how the tower would have looked many years ago to anyone entering after nightfall.

PAST MIDNIGHT, SUNDAY, MAY 10,1863

Marthe ran along the edge of the path, keeping clear of the shells. If Randolph heard her, if he found her dressed for travel, carrying a valise . . . Was Timothy there yet? An owl hooted, and her heart thudded even harder. She reached the tower and opened the door. It was so dark and silent inside. She pulled the door to and took a candle from the valise. After lighting it, she put it in a wall sconce and huddled beside the door. Timothy would come soon and . . . The door opened, and he came in, and she flew thankfully into his arms. She felt the prickle of his beard against her face; then there was nothing in the world but her and Timothy.They never heard the door open.For one last instant, she was in the circle of his arms. Then she heard Randolph's shout as he pulled her away. He raised the dueling pistol and aimed it at Timothy's heart. With a desperate sob, she threw herself between them.

CHAPTER FIFTEEN

The wind moaned through crevices in the old tower. Irregular splotches of damp marked the walls where boards had warped and fingers of rain had poked through. The wooden floor was uneven, buckled with age. A smell of decay, wood rot and dust hung heavily in the dank, close air.

Leah studied the flooring, then crossed to the curving stairway. A gigantic curtain of cobwebs floated mistily across the stairs. No one had climbed these steps in years. She turned back to the octagonal room. She found nothing until she looked on the underside of the stairs and saw a closet door. A chain and a padlock barred access to it.

She jammed the crowbar behind the staple, and the metal piece fell away. Slowly, she opened the closet door. A trunk sat inside, and she pried up its lid. When she saw the contents, a prickle of coldness moved down her back. She lifted out shimmering white folds of silk that were tacked to a box kite.

Seen from a distance the cleverly crafted object certainly looked like the wavering, milky-white gleam of a ghostly figure. The Whispering Lady had been found. Close at hand, the silk was bedraggled, worn at the edges, stained with dirt.

She sighed and bent to replace the silk-bedecked kite. As she did, she saw the outlines of a trapdoor. Shoving the trunk out of the way, she knelt and searched for a finger hole.

A current of air, fresh and damp, stirred her hair, curled like a cat around her ankles, fed the burning wick of the lantern.

A shoe scuffed on the wooden flooring.

Her heart began to thud, and she looked around cautiously.

Cissy stood in the doorway of the closet, hugging her arms tightly against her body. "The floor's dangerous, Leah." She leaned forward, her eyes enormous in her white face. "What are you doing here?"

"You didn't throw my parents' bodies into the river, did you?" Leah demanded, her voice high. "They're somewhere in this tower."

Cissy stared at her, then shifted her eyes to the box kite with its silk hangings. "Just like Mary Ellen, aren't you? So clever to figure things out." She spoke almost in a conversational tone, but it held a metallic edge. "That's what happened, you know. She found my prop." Cissy nodded toward the glistening folds of white. "She knew then that either John Edward or I was The Whispering Lady. I suppose she knew it was me from the first. John Edward would never have been clever enough to plan it all. Anyway, Mary Ellen came up to the house and insisted I go to the tower with her. Then she showed me the ghost figure and accused me of trying to kill Aunt Carrie."

Leah stared up at Cissy's lovely, impassive face, at the deadly green eyes watching her without a flicker of emotion.

"Cissy . . ."

"She was a fool. She said if I left Devereaux Plantation and promised never to come back, she wouldn't tell anyone." Her mouth thinned. "She said she'd protect me." Cissy glared down at Leah. "You do see, don't you? Mary Ellen brought everything on herself with her arrogance, trying to send me away."

"Grandmother took you in and made a home for you. Why did you try to kill her?"

"That was Mary Ellen's fault, too," Cissy said bitterly. "If she had married John Edward, everything would have been all right. I wouldn't have been mistress of Devereaux Plantation, but I could have been sure of my place forever. I could always make John Edward do what I wanted him to." She paused, then said querulously, "I didn't want to hurt Aunt Carrie. She had disinherited Mary Ellen, but I was afraid she might change her mind and that someday Mary Ellen and Tom would inherit Devereaux Plantation, and I would have to leave."

Leah stared at her in horrified fascination. "How could it matter that much to you?"

"Why, I couldn't leave the plantation. Hal couldn't live anywhere but in Mefford County. The Winfreys have always lived in Mefford County." She was trying to make Leah understand. "And that was when Hal had first started coming to see me. If I'd gone away, I would have lost him."

She didn't say outright that Hal had come as much for Devereaux Plantation and the Devereaux name as for her. She had murdered three people and tried to kill three more, all for the love of a weak, idle aristocrat.

Before Leah could grasp the import of what Cissy was doing, the woman had pulled the trunk close to her and put her hand inside. It came out holding a long-barreled dueling pistol.

Cissy pointed the pistol directly at Leah, her eyes blank, her face a rigid mask. Leah's throat tightened. She knew that death was very close.

"Cissy, why did you kill Tom?" she asked desperately.

For a long moment, the pistol remained raised, aimed at her face; then Cissy lowered it just a fraction. "He found us in the tower. He had come looking for Mary Ellen. I tried to make him think she had killed herself like Marthe had done, but he wouldn't believe me. Then it all came to me so quickly, what to do," Cissy continued with a perverse kind of pride. "Because of Marthe, you know. So I shot Tom, then dragged Mary Ellen's body over near his and put the gun in her hand. It looked just right."

The rest had been easy. She'd run to the boat and managed to convince Louisa that Mary Ellen had shot Tom, then killed herself. She'd said Tom had discovered that Mary Ellen and John Edward had planned the ghostly appearances so that Mary Ellen would have an excuse to return to Devereaux Plantation and John Edward. Louisa Shaw, after all, hadn't known Mary Ellen before the boat trip, and there was Mary Ellen's cousin, grief-stricken and horrified, telling Louisa that her daughter-in-law had always been odd and violent-tempered. Cissy had sworn she was willing to do anything to keep the awful truth from Aunt Carrie and protect Leah.

Evil. Easy and evil and successful for so long, Leah thought. "You must have been delighted when it was assumed that The New Star was lost at sea. Then you were safe, weren't you?"

Cissy reached up and pressed her forehead. "Everything was perfect. Aunt Carrie went to Nice, and I was mistress of Devereaux Plantation. Then Hal and I were married. Everything was perfect until this spring."

Spring, and a bearded archaeologist poking here and there, interested in the old tower and wanting to dig.

"My parents are here, under the tower, aren't they?" Leah said.

Cissy nodded. "Old Jason buried them. It was an awful night . . . the wind howling, the rain coming in great waves. We had to use lanterns that night, too." She glanced at the lantern, which was casting its uneven orange light against the walls. Then she looked back at Leah and raised the pistol.

Leah's breath clotted in her chest. She knew what was coming, and there was nothing she could do to stop Cissy.

How would Cissy twist Leah's disappearance to fit the old and tragic stories? Would she suggest to Carrie that Leah had been maddened by the storm that brought back so vividly its echoes of Mary Ellen and Tom's disappearance? Would she suggest that Leah had walked down to the dock and fallen into the raging river?

Mrs. LeClerc had said that Leah had a fated face. Perhaps she was fated to die violently, as her mother and Marthe had died. . . .

The door to the tower slammed open. Merrick stepped inside, water dripping from his yellow sou' wester.

"I'll be damned. I thought I saw a faint glow from the tower . . ." His voice trailed away. He stared at his sister, at the gun in her hand and at Leah's fear blanched face. "What the hell?"

Cissy half turned. "Merrick, you've got to help me. You've got to."

He understood. Abruptly, he understood. He looked at her and tried to speak, but no words came out.

"Merrick, it's her fault," she rushed on, waving the gun at Leah. "She's just like Mary Ellen. And she's treated you just like Mary Ellen treated John Edward. You were fool enough to fall in love with her—then she just danced away, chasing after that archaeologist. I saw it happen."

His face hardened. "Shut up, Cissy."

"But she did. And we can repay her—and get rid of her. Then Devereaux Plantation will be ours, and you can be sure of Ashwood—"

"Cissy, for God's sake!" he cried.

"Merrick, we don't have any choice," she said, as if speaking to an unreasonable child.

"She killed my parents," Leah told him. "They're buried under the tower. And Cissy's been the ghost all these times. She tried to kill Grandmother and Kent and me. . . ."

Now the gun pointed unwaveringly at Leah's head.

"Cissy," Merrick spoke quietly, soothingly. "Give me the gun. I'll take you in to see Dr. Raymond. He'll know what to do."

She stared at him with glittering eyes and took a step back from the closet, nearer to the center of the room. She moved the pistol, and now it was pointed midway between Merrick and Leah.

"No." Sweat beaded her face. Her eyes darted back and forth, from the trunk to the stairway to Merrick.

Leah understood what was happening before he did, and a great rush of grief flooded her. Once again, Cissy was thinking of that old story and the girl who'd shot her lover and then herself. But Leah couldn't bear it if anything happened to Merrick.

Cissy looked at her. "Just like Mary Ellen," she said hoarsely. "Just like Mary Ellen." She plunged across the few feet separating them and jammed the barrel of the weapon against Leah's head.

"Cissy—no—no. Merrick started forward.

"Stop."

A single word, but he understood and stopped.

"Stay there." Cissy smiled. "It will be just like Mary Ellen." Then her face twisted. "Merrick, why do you have to be with her? Don't you see, she's against us. We can put her down there, you and I, and no one will—"

"Cissy, what's going on here? I saw a light coming out of the tower door, and I thought perhaps there was a fire." Hal stood just inside the doorway. Then he saw the gun in Cissy's hand, jammed against Leah's head.

He looked so urbane in his pale blue slacks and navy blue trench coat, a spatter of rain glistening in his blond hair. For the first time, Leah saw a flash of feeling in his face. "Cissy . . ." He said her name with distaste. It was as if he'd caught her out in some unpardonable breach of etiquette.

Merrick moved gingerly, but the old wooden floor creaked. The pistol swung away from Leah, toward him.

"Stop." Hysteria edged Cissy's voice. She waggled the gun between Merrick and Leah. "Hal," she said feverishly, "I need you. You can help me. It will all work out just like it did before. We can put them under the tower, and later we'll sprinkle lime. Or we can set the tower on fire. That's what we'll do, and no one will ever—"

"What are you talking about, Cissy?" Hal's voice was cold and distant.

"She killed Mary Ellen and Tom Shaw years ago," Merrick said. "And now she intends to kill Leah and me."

Hal looked from Merrick to his wife, and his face changed. A withdrawn, dismissive expression settled over it before he shook his head as if in denial.

Cissy's mouth sagged. Her eyes became wild, tormented. "Hal! Hal!"

Hal turned away and walked out into the storm.

Cissy took one step, then she plunged out into the night, calling his name over and over.

"Hal, come back! Hal!"

CHAPTER SIXTEEN

The police didn't find Cissy that night. Her body washed ashore a week later. True to the closemouthed tradition of the South, the real story never came out. Instead, everyone spoke of the sad accident that had befallen Cissy Winfrey the night of the big storm. Whispers floated through Mefford about The Whispering Lady and the tragic Devereaux legacy.

Leah and Merrick gently told Carrie the truth. She insisted it be kept within the family. Brutal as the truth was, Leah felt that her grandmother was now at peace with her memories of Mary Ellen.

Kent Ellis agreed to explore the tower, so it was he who discovered the remains of Mary Ellen and Tom. That caused a flurry of publicity and speculation, but the family made no comment.

The excavations in the tower revealed something else, too, when the sheriff brought a rotted valise to Leah. "Odd thing is, Miss Leah, it's packed for a trip—with women's things."

The Bible was on top. Leah carried it to a table in the library and opened it. She was curious, but she never expected to find what she did—a final entry in the marriage records, written in Marthe's unformed handwriting. The date wasn't filled in, but Leah understood.

Thanking the sheriff, she took the Bible upstairs to show it to her grandmother.

"Don't you see, Grandmother, Marthe was packed and ready to run away with Timothy! She knew they were going to be married, so she entered it in the Bible but left the date blank to fill in later. That means she loved him. She was going to go with him that night . . ."

"And someone stopped them," the old lady finished. "It must have been Randolph."

"Oh, I'm so glad!" Leah cried.

Her grandmother looked at her in surprise.

"Oh, no, I'm not glad they were killed, but I'm so glad she loved Timothy, that she wasn't twisted and hateful."

Smiling, Carrie Devereaux reached for Leah's hand. "I'm glad, too."

Now Leah could look in the mirror, see her face and Marthe's and Mary Ellen's, and smile. She would have smiled a lot if her heart hadn't ached so furiously.

Everyone was kind. Mrs. LeClerc came to call and squeezed her hands. Even John Edward made his peace with her. Several days after Cissy's funeral, he came to her door.

"May I talk with you for a moment?" He rubbed his jaw with his knuckles. "Let's take a walk."

They went down the oyster-shell path through the rose gardens. At the wooden bridge, he looked at her directly. "I didn't know. I hope you'll believe that."

When she looked into his eyes, she knew he was telling her the truth. She reached out and took his hand. "I do—and I'm sorry about Cissy. I'm really very sorry."

He bit his lip, then said huskily, "I believe you, too. Cissy . . . she was such a pretty little girl. But I think she was always afraid after our folks died. She wanted so much to feel safe." He took a deep breath. "Maybe she's safe now." He patted Leah clumsily on the shoulder. "At least you care. I don't think Hal's given it any thought at all."

"That's probably not fair. He must be terribly upset."

"All he seemed to care about was being sure all of his family stuff was moved back to the Winfrey house in town." He shook his head. "Anyway, he's gone, and I'll be gone soon, too."

"Gone?"

"I'm going to rent a place in town."

"No!"

He was startled at her vehemence.

"No, John Edward. You mustn't leave. Grandmother depends upon you." Her voice softened. "She loves you."

"You don't mind if I stay?" he asked uncertainly.

"I want you to stay."

Slowly, he smiled. "I can't tell you what this means to me. We'll take care of Aunt Carrie together." Then, as he turned to go, he asked, "Have you talked to Merrick yet?"

"No."

"Go see him."

She watched John Edward's broad back disappear up the path.

Go see him.

Oh, she wanted to. She wanted to very much.

She thought about that wonderful afternoon at Ashwood, the warmth of Merrick's touch, the feel of his mouth on hers.

She ran toward the garage. As she climbed into the Vega and backed it out, she could see Merrick's face: loving, angry, hurt, brave. She drove fast, too fast, and dust boiled up behind the car as she ascended the last hill to Ashwood. After she braked beside the station wagon, her courage deserted her. How could he ever forgive her?

Then she thought of her mother and Marthe.

She found him behind the house in the garden, spading a flower bed. He looked wonderful, with sweat staining the front of his shirt, with dirt on his hands where he'd picked weeds. He turned toward her. At first he seemed surprised and eager, but then his expression became distant.

"Hal's moved into town," she said.

"Really?"

"Yes. And John Edward was going to move, too, but I asked him to stay. Someone needs to be in charge and take care of Grandmother. And John Edward will want to oversee Kent's excavations. He has lots more planned."

Merrick homed in on one particular sentence. "Why does John Edward need to take care of Aunt Carrie? I thought you would do that."

"Of course I will. And you will, too. But someone should actually be on the spot."

He stared at her. "Where will you be?"

"At Ashwood—if you'll have me."

He was silent for a long moment.

"Can't you forgive me? I always wanted to believe you loved me, but it's hard to accept magic. I didn't know why you would care about me—"

"Care about you?" he said roughly. "I want you more than anything in the world."

"Take me."

He moved quickly, and she was in his arms. Her mouth sought his, and warmth and happiness and the beginnings of desire flamed within her.

This, then, was the Devereaux legacy: to love passionately and well.

ABOUT THE AUTHOR

CAROLYN HART is the author of forty-seven mysteries. New in 2012 is *Death Comes Silently*, twenty-second in the Death on Demand series. Hart's books have won Agatha, Anthony, and Macavity awards. She has twice appeared at the National Book Festival in Washington, DC. She is thrilled that some of her long-ago books are having a new life. She lives in Oklahoma City with her husband, Phil. She loves mysteries, cats, happy ghosts, Oklahoma, and South Carolina.